MAVERICKS:
CHARLIE PARR'S GUNSMOKE CURE

LONGRIDERS OF THE WEST ™
MAVERICKS

LANCE CLAYTON•DOC GRIMSON•CHARLIE PARR•LOCKJAW JOHNSON•FLINT MADDOX

CHARLIE PARR'S GUNSMOKE CURE

By Kent Thorn

POPULAR PUBLICATIONS • 2018

PUBLISHING HISTORY

"Charlie Parr's Gunsmoke Cure" originally appeared in the February 1935 issue of
Bull's-Eye Western Stories magazine (Vol. 1, No. 1). Copyright 1935, 1962 by Popular
Publications, Inc. All Rights Reserved.

CHAPTER 1
BLOOD ON THE MOON

CHARLIE PARR'S white mustache drooped moodily with the down-curve of his mouth, but his keen, ageless blue eyes, set in the wrinkled leather of his face, showed a glint of reluctant admiration.

"Now that," he said glumly, "is what I call trailin'!"

Doc Grimson, lying next to him, nodded. "I'm getting so I'd hardly take anything for that jasper," he remarked. "He's added more to the gaiety of life these past two weeks than anybody else has for two years."

His mobile, expressive features, with their curious mingling of strength and sensitiveness, were cool and a little sardonic, but his luminous gray eyes danced with a genuine, almost child-like pleasure.

Flint Maddox forebodingly eyed the tiny mounted figure far below them. "Just the same," he remarked, "I've got a hunch that life ain't goin' to be so gay before he gets through. Plenty of good men are breaking rock because they thought they was smarter than Slag McLeod."

Lance Clayton grinned, teeth white against the lean, hard-fleshed tan of his face. "Lay you two to one in blues he takes the down canyon to the left."

Lockjaw Johnson thought that over. "I'll bet with you, Lance," he said finally. "Only I ain't got no blue chip on me."

1

Charlie Parr snorted. "Ain't anybody got any kind of chips," he said morosely.

Lance Clayton turned his eyes and his thoughts back to Slag McLeod and his ant-like, solitary progress over the trail below.

At that distance, nearly half a mile straight down, he appeared to be moving with painful slowness. It made him somehow all the more impressive—his doggedness, his patient skill in unraveling sign, the sheer guts of his trailing alone after five such men as they were.

This Slag McLeod, U.S. Marshal, hadn't gotten his reputation for nothing—that was sure. For two weeks, Charlie Parr had put everything he knew into trying to cover their trail, and what Charlie didn't know about that wasn't in the book. Yet the man below them had solved, with startling ease, the toughest problems Charlie had put up to him. He never appeared to hurry but somehow he was always there, just a little behind them—dogged, tireless, menacing.

Lance had seen the man once—a lean, gray, quiet man, with hard eyes and thin lips and a body that gave the impression of being made of rawhide and tempered steel. When he had first taken their trail, after the train hold-up, the Five Mavericks had considered it a good game. McLeod had led his posse well. It had taken all their wits to get away from him. When the posse had finally thinned out during the long chase until only McLeod was left, they had laughed. But since then it had gotten past being a joke. Slag McLeod had begun to get on their nerves.

"I'm tired of bein' chased to hell and back by this here tinhorn star-toter," said Lockjaw with sudden sullenness. "If he don't git throwed off this time, let's wait an' trim his horns."

Charlie Parr growled: "We'd have to kill him. Ain't it enough for you to have the federal government on our trail, without gittin' 'em buzzin' after us for murderin' one of their men?"

"I didn't mean to dry-gulch him, Charlie," Lockjaw said. "It ain't murder to shoot it out with a gent, fair."

"Who are you goin' to git for witnesses, you dumb galoot? It'd be murder as far as the gov'ment's concerned."

"They don't know it was us that robbed that train," Lockjaw argued stubbornly. "How are they goin' to prove it was us that ventilated him?"

Doc Grimson smiled. "They don't know," he cut in softly, "but they're doing plenty of guessing. We'd better cherish this Slag McLeod like a brother."

Lance saw that the lone figure below them had dismounted and was slowly and methodically scanning the rock ahead of him. After a moment he stood up and cast a look around at the high ground where the Five perched. Lance held his breath. He had an idea that the eyes of that gray man down there could look through bushes and distance, could search them out even through solid rock. But the gaze swept past them, then returned to the rock ahead of him.

Charlie Parr had deliberately left sign there—sign so minute and insignificant that it might not have been noticed by anyone but Slag McLeod. And that sign led to a rock-floored canyon which split into a hundred draws and gullies and side-canyons, up any one of which five men might go without leaving trace of their passing. But the Five had not gone down where the sign led. They had circled to the right, also on rock, taking a trail which was more fit for mountain goats than for even such horses as they had. And Charlie Parr had carefully removed all small traces of their passing.

Lance's pulses began to pound with excitement. For the marshal, after having cast about like a hound at fault, had obviously found the false trail they had left him. Instead of taking it, however, he had gone over and was scanning the steep, broken slope up which they had ridden. After a moment, he turned back his horse, with a gesture of decision, and—took the trail down canyon!

Lance let out his breath softly. In the others, tension relaxed visibly.

Charlie Parr got to his feet in a movement of vigorous determination. "And now," he growled grimly, "we're goin' to stick up a bank!"

Lance laughed a little. Charlie was good and sore, all right, and Lance couldn't altogether blame him. The outlaw business had been pretty unprofitable for them, and Charlie had gotten mighty tired of it.

Charlie Parr had been outside the law for some forty years. Once a member of Boot Hill Kennedy's gang, he had gun-quarrelled with that famous bandit over the latter's habit of promiscuous killing. With Kennedy's resultant demise, Charlie had become leader of the gang but resigned, accompanied by the faithful Lockjaw Johnson, when the boys voted that he was not hard-boiled enough for the job.

After some lone-wolf years, he had encountered Doc Grimson and with Lance and Flint Maddox, had formed that gang known as the Five Mavericks, noted from Border to Border as the most brilliant and daring of all the groups that rode the Owlhoot Trail. They were an unusual bunch, just as likely to prey on other outlaws as on the ruthless rich within the fold of respectability. And more than once they had even forgotten the job they had in hand in order to lend their guns and lives to some one who needed help.

The result was a lot of reputation but comparatively little cash.

And it was against this circumstance that Charlie Parr had

revolted. He would maybe get old some day, he declared, and the others weren't getting any younger. He didn't propose to end his days as a saddle bum. Now was the time to lay up some cash. So they had set out to stick up a bank.

Unfortunately, unexpected events had intervened. They had ended by achieving a brilliant train robbery in the interest of a widow-lady in distress and had again taken the trail without profit to themselves. Doc Grimson had thought it wiser not to have the federal government down on them, so they had confined their robbery to the packet which concerned the fate of the widow and passed up the rest of the mail. That fact, however, had not kept Slag McLeod off their trail.

"An' this time," Charlie gritted, glaring, "if any lop-eared, bug-eyed piece of sucker meat amongst you tries to git off the trail on account of some galoot that's in trouble, I'm gonna kiss him on the cabeza with a six-gun barrel!"

He pointed over the bulge of the ridge on which they stood. "Yonder," he said, "about fifty miles, lies Jugtown. There's a bank there with plenty of money in it. Let's go!"

Doc Grimson whistled softly. "You like 'em tough, don't you?"

"What's this here Jugtown?" inquired Lockjaw, to whom one town was like another, particularly if it had a bank.

"The denizens of that there burg," Lance Clayton volunteered solemnly, "are so pi'zen that just the smell of 'em has killed off all the rattlers for miles around."

Lockjaw began to feel that he was being kidded. "Where I come from," he said with a slow grin, "there ain't no rattlers neither. One time one of 'em bit one of the children. It give him hydrophobia an' he went around bitin' all the other rattlers, until the country was clean of 'em."

Lance whooped. "When Lockjaw gits to thinkin' up comebacks like that, there's blood on the moon!"

CHAPTER 2
OUTSKIRTS OF HELL

THERE WAS blood on it two mornings later as they threaded their way through a maze of arroyos which crisscrossed the flats leading to Jugtown. They had let the horses rest one whole day and then had gone on at night. It was nearly dawn when the shooting began and the moon was setting, red and ominous on the far horizon.

The shots came from some distance away, a brisk fusillade, lacing the dim red glow of the night with gun-fire.

"Looks like somebody was havin' a party," Lance remarked, nose up.

"No you don't!" Charlie Parr snapped impatiently. "We ain't hornin' in on this here ruckus none whatever!"

Lance relaxed, disappointed. "We could just amble over an' see what's happening, couldn't we?"

But it appeared that they were to see, anyway. The night was suddenly vibrant with the beat of hoofs, and they could make out a single rider, apparently chased by a number of others, and coming in their direction. About fifty yards from them, however, the first rider's mount went down. The man himself hit the ground rolling, twisted to his feet with a lithe, cat-like movement and jumped for the scant shelter of some nearby rocks. Once there, his six-guns began a staccato, flaming roll which emptied one saddle. His pursuers flung themselves from their mounts and sought cover.

But it was plain enough that the man there behind the rocks was doomed. There were almost a dozen men ringing him. It would not be long before they closed in. The victim realized it, for he suddenly called out: "Come ahead, *amigitos míos!* Come and see how a *caballero* of Chihuahua can die!"

Lance Clayton started. "Now where have I heard—" he began to mutter, then his voice cracked out, "Ricky! Is that you, Ricky, *mío? Cómo to pasa, amigito?*" he called. "How's it going, pardner?"

There was an instant of apparently astonished silence from the rocks—an instant in which the attackers' fire ceased, as though they also had been stunned into silence by this voice from the arroyo rim. Then a relieved chuckle came from the rocks. *"Ola! Nino!* I theenk it goes very well *ahora,"* Then in Spanish, "The voice of an old friend is like a draught of wine to the heart."

"This hombre a friend of yours, Lance?" Flint asked swiftly. He sounded even more relieved than the man behind the rocks.

"I'll say!" said Lance jubilantly.

Doc Grimson's chuckle sounded joyous. Charlie Parr swore. "He would be!"

"Hey, you fellers," he called. "The game's up. We're givin' you three seconds to get to your horses."

"The hell you say!" a voice snarled, and a bullet hummed near Charlie's shoulder.

Lance Clayton's six-guns blasted the night with twin slashes of bellowing flame. Beside them, Doc and Charlie's Colts beat staccato counterpoint; then came Flint's thunder and the deadly hammering of Lockjaw's gun.

A MAN in front cried out, loomed up briefly and hit ground again with a slithering thud. The Five were off their horses now, running forward, ripping the ground ahead with lead like recurrent gusts of hail. It was too much for the gang in front. They broke suddenly, leapt for their horses, and pounded away.

Doc and Charlie closed in on the three blotches which lay still against the earth where the attackers had been. Lance, reloading his gun, started to walk back toward the rocks, but a voice from the side halted him. *"Aqui estoy, amigo mío*—Here I am, my friend."

Lance grinned. "Who were your little playmates?"

"That is something I would like to know," the Mexican said. "They don't theenk to introduce themselves biffore the party."

Together they walked over to where Doc and the others were. One of the men on the ground was groaning, and Doc Grimson knelt by his side. He was a Mexican, and Ricky, asked him in Spanish: "Who sent you on this devil's work, hombre?"

The man on the ground stopped groaning only long enough to spit defiantly and gasp, "Ah! *Madre de Dios,* I am dying."

And, shortly, he did. The other two, were already dead. One was an American, but Lance's Mexican friend, whom he introduced as Ricardo Perez y Gonzales, had never seen either of the three before.

When Doc Grimson had dressed the wound in his shoulder,

he explained as much as he knew of the fight. "You know," he began with an ingratiating grin. "This Jogtown—he is jost by the Border. I theenk, thees is ver' good place to make a leetle what you call smoggling—no? But someone here, he don' like that. I get nice leetle letter. Thees letter, she say, 'You've come to the wrong place, hombre. Git, while you're still healt'y.' But I am liking thees contry ver' moch. I don' go."

"There's about as much scare in this crazy Spick as there is in a creased bob-cat," Lance said. "Him an' me did some ridin' together below the line an' I know—hey, Ricky?"

Ricardo Perez y Gonzales grinned at the others. "He is call' me crazy, thees *nino,* biccause I am not ron when he get us into trobble.... We must go back now an' look for my men. I do not theenk thees is useful, but I must go see. There was three of us. I am hit but once, in the shoulder, like you see—biccause I move ver' queek. These others I theenk we fin' them ver' dead. Someone weel pay me moch, I theenk—for thees night!"

They found that it was as Ricardo had suspected. His men were both dead, and the saddle bags of Ricardo's dead horse were empty. The Five Mavericks asked no questions about what had been in them. And Ricardo said nothing.

It was Charlie Parr who said brusquely, "Well, we'd better be gettin' along. I reckon our friend here is all right now."

Lance asked with concern: "Can you get back without runnin' into these jaspers, Ricky?"

"But yes, *amigito,*" the Mexican answered quickly. He was already mounted on one of the dead men's horses which Lance had roped for him. Now he swept off his high-peaked, jingling sombrero in a wide, courteous gesture. *"Adios, Señores,"* he said. "I am weeshing you good lock, but also that the saints will geeve me one chance to return a leetle of w'at I owe."

"Well, anyway," remarked Charlie Parr with a relieved sigh as the other disappeared, "that came out all right. Now we can get at that bank!"

CHAPTER 3
THE JUGTOWN BULL

LON CARMODY cheerfully said, "Go tie it on, Josh," as the bank's elderly-cashier announced his intention of going to lunch. He tried, as always recently, to keep the pity out of his voice, but he could not keep it out of his eyes as he watched Josh Venner's listless figure descend the steps and disappear on its way to the dining room of the Jugtown Hotel.

Josh Venner had once been president and chief stockholder of the bank and a big man in Jugtown. That had been before the advent of Canuck Bull. Now Josh Venner was a broken old man, glad to have a poorly-paid job as cashier in the bank he had once owned. And Lon Carmody, twenty-three, husky and good-looking, understood broken men. He was one himself.

There had been a time when he, like Venner, had held himself with some pride. He was a good hand with cattle, could sit some pretty tough broncs, and, though he had never done any killing, he wasn't such a slow hand with a six-gun. That also had been *before* the advent of Canuck Bull.

There had been a time—just one unforgettable time—when

12

he had tried to go up against Canuck Bull, when the latter had just come to Jugtown and began to run the blaze which had later made him boss of the place. Lon hadn't been scared at all to begin with. The quarrel had come quickly and his temper had flared up. Before he knew just what was happening he had been jockied into a spot where he had had to go for his gun, and he had gone for it. He remembered now, as he had remembered a thousand searing times since then, the sudden sickness that came into his stomach when he saw that he had lost the play, that his draw was too slow.

No doubt he had had it in his mind that the big, loud-mouthed man before him was something of a four-flusher. Certainly, he had expected nothing like the lightning, unerring flick of the big hand to the holstered gun. His own gun had not yet cleared leather when the muzzle of the other's .45 was trained on his stomach.

Often, since then, he had tried to figure out why he had been suddenly so terrified. It seemed to him that Canuck Bull had somehow gotten the jump on him, mentally. A few ill-natured words had developed into a shooting affair with such blasting suddenness. He tried to tell himself that if he had had more time, he'd have behaved better.

And then there was something in Canuck Bull's manner that had kind of stampeded him—his voice, loud, harsh, driving— the sudden, aggressive ferocity in his face and manner, that hadn't even a vestige of bluff about it. He realized that it had shaken him, even in the instant when he drove for his gun. But he hadn't really lost his nerve until that Colt was trained on his middle and he realized that he didn't have a chance—not a mortal chance! It would have been better if he had gone on with his draw then, and died. But he hadn't been able to.

And Canuck Bull had seen his fear! Lon remembered how his eyes had glittered with a kind of cruel, contemptuous triumph. Slowly, he had elevated the muzzle of his gun, until it centered between Lon's eyebrows. And still he was unable to move his gun-hand—as helpless to move any part of his body as a rabbit under the spell of a rattler. Uncomprehending, he watched the muzzle of the Colt move aside a little. Then the gun went off.

DEAFENED, HE felt something sting his left ear. And still he hadn't moved. It wasn't so much fear now, as it was astonishment. He had expected to be dead and he wasn't altogether sure that he wasn't until he heard Canuck Bull's bellow of laughter. The big man had bolstered his Colt and caught Lon's gun-hand and wrenched the gun away from it.

"You yeller whelp!" he had bellowed. "I'll teach you to try to stand up against a *man!*" The barrel of Lon's own Colt smashed unexpectedly against Lon's face. He staggered back, his hands going instinctively to his face, so that he had no warning of the attack which followed. Canuck Bull had tossed the gun aside after that first blow. Now his big fist crashed with stunning force into Lon's face. Lon staggered back, falling. Canuck Bull yanked him to his feet, smashed pile-driver blows to his body.

Belatedly, Lon had tried to cover, to save himself. It meant merely that he had stayed on his feet to take more punishment. He was rushed from one end of the room to the other, knocked down, picked up, battered against the wall until he was sick and dizzy. That beating seemed to him endless. He did not even try to fight back. It would have been useless—he was too dazed after the first blow. But in his heart he knew that what dazed him as much as the blows was the bewildering ferocity of the thing—the stark, savage cruelty of it.

Most of it was just a haze. He remembered clearly being on the floor and being kicked, felt the crushing thud of a boot tear his ribs loose, then a kick must have landed under his breastbone because he lost consciousness.

When he came to, it was to a nightmare. A whirl of garish lights and hazy forms circled about him. A voice, like that of a soul in torment, groaned in his ears. For a moment he thought it was his own voice, but then things settled down a little and he saw that Shorty Meldrum lay near him, in a welter of blood. Even in the hell of pain which racked his body, he realized that Shorty was dying. And Shorty was his partner.

He didn't have to be told what had happened. Somehow, he knew that Shorty hadn't been able to see him kicked that way, had tried to draw against Canuck Bull. And what he, Lon, had somehow escaped, Shorty had gotten. Shorty had taken a .45 slug in the stomach. It took him a good while to die, and it was not nice to watch. Lon, who was unable to move, saw it all.

After that, there were days of semiconsciousness and delirium, during which he watched Shorty die over and over again. Days when he himself lay between life and death, with a fractured skull, and several broken ribs, one of which had punctured a lung.

The doctor had warned him that he ought not to ride for at least a year. He never had tried to ride again, but he knew that it wasn't because of what the doctor said. It was because he could not face the boys on the spread any more. Nobody had told him that it was up to him to go after Canuck Bull and get him for killing Shorty Meldrum. A man didn't have to be told that. But when he thought of facing that big killer again, something in him just curled up and quit. He had tried a thousand times to whip himself up to it, but he knew all the while that he was only fooling himself. So Lon avoided him.

He would have left town if it hadn't been for Jane Venner. Jane was Josh Venner's niece. She had made her uncle give Lon a place in the bank and she had insisted on Lon's taking it. It meant that he could at least be in the same town with Jane.

Not that that would do him any good. He would never be able to ask a girl like her to marry a thing like himself, and even if he did, she'd never accept him. He couldn't even dream of her until he had faced Canuck Bull—and facing Canuck Bull was something which was also not to be dreamed of. It was hopeless. He was licked, and he knew it.

STEPS IN the doorway caused him to look up from the brooding into which Venner's departure had thrown him. Three men stood there—three men whose faces were covered by bandannas and who held six-guns in their hands.

"Don't move your hands from that counter," one of them warned in a curiously cold, resonant voice.

The three robbers advanced on him briskly. One came directly to the window of his cage and rested the hand holding his gun on the counter; the other two came toward him behind the counter.

The man in front of Lon was big-shouldered and slim-waisted and must have stood over six feet in his socks. Lon got the impression, somehow, that he was young, though there was nothing especially young about the expression of the eyes underneath the sombrero.

"Just take it easy and don't move." The voice had the chill of ice in it.

Vaguely, Lon was aware that the other two had come around behind them and had squatted down beside him.

The man who had spoken first said: "Come ahead—*nino*." There was a faint overtone of irony in his voice.

The third man, who had not yet spoken, said gruffly: "If anybody comes in don't try to give the game away. I'll be watching you and you'll just get yourself and him killed. Now, open that safe."

Lon moved his head, carefully, as though his neck were fragile, and looked down at the man who spoke. Again the eyes which met his were blue and menacing, but this time they were set in a fine network of wrinkles. And the few strands of hair visible between the mask and the sombrero were white.

"I don't know the combination."

It was perfectly true. Venner kept the combination and locked the safe when he went out for lunch. Lon had only a small amount of silver and bills in his drawer with which to meet any checks presented during lunch hour.

The eyes which looked into his went several degrees colder.

17

"You'd better try to remember it," the man said in a voice which matched his look. And for the second time in his life, Lon Carmody decided that he was a dead man.

"I swear to God that only the cashier knows it," he said in a whisper.

For a second the other said nothing and Lon held his breath. Then the man with the oddly vibrant voice said: "Never mind. I think he's telling the truth."

He got up and went over and knelt down before the safe door. He took the knob between the thumb and forefinger of the most supple hand Lon had ever seen and put his ear against the lock.

Outside, at the door, a voice which sounded somehow strangled said, "Hey, ma'am! Wh—where you goin'?"

A girl's voice, a little sharp with surprise answered, "I'm going into the bank, of course."

The back of Lon Carmody's neck felt cold. That was Jane Venner's voice.

"Er—er," the voice outside gurgled, with a note of desperation in it. "What—what are you goin' in there for?"

"Are you crazy?" she asked. "What business is it of yours?"

Apparently, the man outside could think of no reply to that. He was silent while the girl started to mount the steps again. Then he found his tongue. "What's the use of doin' that, ma'am?" he got out, pleadingly. "Er—this here bank's closed—er—for lunch." Evidently, he felt that that had been an inspiration, for his voice suddenly sounded relieved and quite confident as he went on. "Yes, *ma'am!* She's plumb closed. Bank folks got to eat like anybody else."

A low, choking sound near him drew Lon's attention and he saw that the big-shouldered young man, who had come around and was crouching with the others behind the counter, had his head down and that his shoulders were shaking in some sort of silent paroxysm. For a second he didn't understand. Then he realized with amazement that the man was laughing.

From the long moment of silence outside, it was evident that Jane Venner was staring at the fourth man in outraged astonishment. Suddenly her voice came, full of indignant contempt. "You must be drunk!" Then her trim figure appeared in the doorway and her light, firm, decided steps began to cross the open space before the counter. Behind her, one of the oddest men Lon Carmody had ever seen lurched hastily into view. He was a big man, with a huge barrel chest. His face was unmasked and looked harassed, bewildered, doggone abashed, and indignant. At the sight of that stranger's face and that great chest and awkward shamble, some vague impression stirred in Lon's mind.

Jane Venner turned sharply in her tracks. "Are you following me?" she demanded dangerously.

The big man behind her had been staring around the bank in a bewildered way. Helplessly, now he caught the expression in the girl's eyes, goggled, shifted from foot to foot, and then turned and went hastily out the door.

Jane Venner swung back toward Lon, the lightning still in her eye. "I never saw a drunk look so sober," she said indignantly. Then her expression changed. "Why, Lon!" she exclaimed, concerned. "What on earth is the matter with you? You look like a ghost."

Lon Carmody's heart jumped fearfully. "Why—I—I guess I don't feel very good," he stuttered. From the corner of his eye, he could glimpse the white-haired man staring at him glacially and the big-shouldered young man with his head up and his eyes alert and wondering. But he forced himself to concentrate all his attention on the girl. He had an idea that it was about the healthiest thing he could do under the circumstances.

THE TELLER had not been mistaken in the expression of Lance Clayton's eyes—Lance found himself at once alert and full of wonder. That girl he couldn't see, there in front of the counter, had the kind of voice you tumbled on once in a coon's age. He had been half-hysterical over Lockjaw's clumsy efforts to keep her from coming in.

It was not until the girl's tone had changed in addressing the teller that the quality of her voice really sobered Lance. It was not only beautifully modulated and melodious, that voice—it had a quality of warmth in it that nestled around the heart like the glow of some ancient golden liquor. Hearing it, you instinctively knew a lot about the girl who possessed it—knew the fire in her but knew too, as though you yourself had experienced it, the treasure of tenderness and loyalty which she could pour out for a man.

Lance scarcely heard what she said—so occupied was he with the mere sound of her voice—until a note of deep indignation in her tone aroused his attention.

"He's made Ed Parker raise my rent so high that I couldn't pay my expenses there even if he hadn't driven away nearly every customer I've got!" the girl was exclaiming bitterly.

"Did—did Ed admit that?" the teller asked nervously.

"Practically," the girl said indignantly. "But Ed didn't need to admit it. By himself, Ed wouldn't play such a trick."

"I—I can't figger why Canuck Bull would have it in for you that way," the teller said hesitantly. "He let Josh stay on here in the bank—an'—an' me, too."

There was a momentary silence, then the teller's voice, embarrassed, with a note of ineffectual anger in it. "He—he hasn't been botherin' you, has he, Jane?"

"Bothering me? The beast!" the girl burst out. "He told me the other day that he could take me any time he wanted to—that the only reason he didn't was because he wanted to make me come to him, for the fun of the thing."

"The dirty skunk! By God, I'll—" the teller's voice choked.

The girl said nothing. Lance Clayton had an idea that she was waiting, in a sort of desperate hopefulness for the teller to go on.

"I—he runs the town, Jane—if I—Jane—wouldn't you let me help you to go away—go with you—"

"Let that brute run me out of my own home town?" the girl flared indignantly.

The teller shrugged his shoulders despairingly. "I'd like to kill him, Jane," he said, without conviction. "Some day—"

The girl broke in on him warmly. "Don't, Lon! Don't think or talk that way. I know—you musn't even think of such a thing.

Lance Clayton measured him coolly then shot
his right hand to Canuck Bull's jaw.

"I know I oughtn't to come here and tell you all this," she
went on, after a moment. "It isn't fair. It's only that—that there's
no one for me to talk to. I couldn't go to Uncle Josh. If he ever

lost his place in the bank—there's Aunt Nellie, you see, and Bob and Nancy—they can scarcely live as it is on the measly little salary Uncle Josh gets. Don't think about it any more, Lon. I was so upset at losing the restaurant. There's simply no other place for it, and nothing else for me to do. Oh! I'll make out— some way. I must go now—" She forced a little musical laugh. "Some stranger that doesn't know any better might come by and want something to eat."

Lance Clayton felt the world shaking under his feet. He had suddenly become aware of two facts, which couldn't possibly go together, but which nonetheless evidently did. The first fact was that the teller called Lon was about as yellow as they came anywhere; the second was that this girl with the deep, warm, tender voice was in love with him!

He heard her feet go down the steps in front of the bank and automatically got to his own feet, oblivious of Charlie Parr's scowl. He had remembered that from where he stood he could no doubt see her pass by one of the front windows. And he had to look at her. There wasn't any way out of that—and if anybody saw his masked face out over the counter, it would be just too bad.

CHAPTER 4
ONE HOUR FROM HELL

LON CARMODY, in the shame and helpless anger which gnawed at him, had almost managed to forget the men—and the guns—crouching at his side. He watched Jane

Venner go through the door of the bank with a wild impulse in him to shout to her to come back—to tell her that he was going out now and rid the world of Canuck Bull or die like a man trying. But the idea was its own antidote. His shoulders drooped again. He hadn't the nerve—he never would have the nerve. And you knew that all the more clearly because Canuck Bull himself appeared on the street outside. Lon could see him clearly, could see Jane Venner when she tried to pass him and brought up angrily when Canuck Bull stretched out his big arm to bar her path.

He could not hear what they were saying, but he could see that Jane was speaking angrily and that Canuck Bull was laughing—a big, careless, bull-necked man, with a deceptive layer of fat over his heavy, cat-like muscles and a kind of overlay of joviality and good-fellowship, which covered his native ferocity.

Then Canuck Bull reached out his great arms and swept the girl against him with a swift irresistible movement and kissed her square on the mouth. Lon Carmody felt like a man on the rack. Fury and hatred blazed up in him like a fever but the fear in him was a greater sickness still.

There was an incredulous exclamation at his side, and suddenly the big-shouldered young man vaulted the counter. Lon saw him snatch off the bandanna mask as he reached the doorway.

What he saw next etched itself on his memory almost as vividly as that night when he himself had, incredibly, bearded Canuck Bull and been beaten into a pulp. He saw a tall, big-shouldered young man, with lean, hard-flesh features and blazing blue eyes, appear at the side of the girl and the big man who still held her, struggling, in his arms.

He saw the young man's hand shoot out and grasp—it was unthinkable!—Canuck Bull's nose between his thumb and forefinger, and twist, hard. Canuck Bull bellowed with pain and rage. He released the girl, slapping furiously at the hand which held his nose. The hand released its grip, and snapped back in a fist, which smacked against Canuck Bull's cheekbone.

Canuck Bull staggered backward and sat down suddenly, the blood spurting from his face. He did not try to get up. Instead, his big paw flashed for his gun in that swift, licking movement which Lon Carmody remembered too well. At the same instant, two other things happened. The foot of the big, barrel-chested, awkward man who had followed Jane into the bank shot out and kicked Canuck Bull's gun from his hand as it cleared leather. The second thing was the appearance in the hand of the young man of a Colt's .45. Lon Carmody blinked. He could have sworn that the big-shouldered young man had not started his draw until after Bull had started his. Yet Lon could have sworn too, that the young man's Colt had appeared, magically, in his hand *before* the barrel-chested hombre had kicked.

AN EXCLAMATION at his elbow brought him out of the daze into which this impossibility had thrown him. It was the white-haired man who spoke. "The danged fool!" he said disgustedly. "What are we supposed to be doin'—rescuin' young females in distress or robbin' a bank?"

"We must remember that we, too, were once young," the

other said in a voice in which weariness, amusement, and irony were nicely blended.

Lon Carmody saw that the big-shouldered young man had re-holstered his gun. Canuck Bull got to his feet and rushed, bellowing. A right and a left to the face stopped him short. His arms dropped a little. The big-shouldered man measured him coolly, then shot his right hand to the jaw. It landed, that punch, like the kick of a mule. Canuck Bull's knees buckled. He hit the ground face forward and lay as still as if he had been pole-axed.

Now, Lon saw the barrel-chested hombre hit one of Canuck Bull's henchmen who tried to draw on the big-shouldered man. The blow looked slow, after the lightning smash of those other fists, but it apparently had the force of an earthquake. The unfortunate gunman ended up fifteen feet away, tangled in the legs of the crowd.

Another of Canuck Bull's gun-slingers tried the same trick. But that magic draw of the big-shouldered man caught him with his gun still in leather.

"Hold it!" The warning cracked out like the snap of a bull-whip. The gunman froze, eased his hand away from the gun-butt as though it were a snake that he was afraid of disturbing. The barrel-chested man's gun was out now—a smooth, slow draw, with an air of unconcerned leisureliness about it, but the ham-like hand which held the gun was rock-like, menacing.

"What you waitin' for, you skunk-smellin' sissies?" inquired the barrel-chested man pugnaciously. "Ain't there nobody else that wants some fun?"

Nobody answered.

Lon saw a lean, wolf-like man with a star on his chest come down the street and head for the center of disturbance. It was U.S. Marshal Slag McLeod!

Evidently, the two men at his elbow knew him, too. The elder gave a baffled exclamation of rage. "There it goes!" he ground out. "That ends it!"

The slender man said: "We'd better get out."

They started to go, but the white-haired man whirled on Lon Carmody suddenly and snarled, "You ain't seen anything—understand? I may be runnin' with a gang of half-wits and nurses for females, but I'm *bad!* Savvy? Plumb cultus pi'sen! If you want to stay healthy, you cultivate a dam' poor memory!"

Looking into the blaze of his eyes, Lon Carmody believed him. He shook a little as he watched the pair go out the back door. When he turned back to the street, he saw that Slag McLeod had pushed his way through the crowd and was standing staring at the two men with guns in their hands.

It was the marshal who spoke first.

"That'll be all," he said. "Put up your gun, Clayton."

Lon Carmody's mind reeled. Clayton! Then complete realization rushed in on him, with the memory, sprung full-grown now, which had started when the barrel-chested man had come into the doorway. Lance Clayton! Lockjaw Johnson! And the others? What a fool he had been not to *know!* They couldn't be anybody in the world but Charlie Parr and Doc Grimson. But that only made four. Where was Flint Maddox? With the horses, of course!

Like everybody else West of Kansas City he knew the legend of the Five Mavericks—had heard their descriptions a thousand times. So familiar to him were they, that he had thought to know them better than his own friends—to know them and love them better—perhaps because they were everything he had dreamed of being and had dismally failed to be—because they represented, for him, all that was glamorous and admirable. And he had failed to recognize them!

THE THOUGHTS raced through his mind in one blinding instant which lasted only the short second it took Lance Clayton to answer Slag McLeod.

"This pole-cat," he indicated Canuck Bull who was slowly writhing into consciousness, "insulted a lady an' took kind of sick of it. I'm tellin' you that so you'll understand the play. Further than that I will state that I generally leather my iron—an' unleather it—when the notion takes me."

Lon Carmody's heart jumped up into his throat. Lance Clayton's tone had been careless, even pleasant, but there was an emphasis on the last words which spoke volumes. He was telling Slag McLeod where to get off. And men who did that were not likely to live long!

The marshal eyed him with more stony expression than ever. "Clayton," he said after a moment, "as far as I'm concerned, you can carry your gun in your hand or hangin' from your nose. There's no law against it. I'm just tellin' you that this partic'lar play is over. An' that goes as it lays."

Lance Clayton grinned suddenly and holstered his gun.

"Slag," he said, his eyes twinkling, "I can't disagree with you about that—I noticed it myself."

Lockjaw Johnson guffawed. "Haw! Haw! Noticed it himself!" Almost immediately, however, he looked sulky. "Danged if this don't beat anything! Folks goes around braggin' that this here town is shore pi'sen. An' when it comes to a showdown, it resembles more a prairie dog village than anythin' I ever—" He broke off, staring at Doc Grimson and Flint Maddox and Charlie Parr, who were making their way through the crowd toward him.

Slag McLeod looked at them through suddenly narrowed eyes. "Where one is, the others aren't far away," he remarked grimly. "It's a funny thing, but I've just come from trailin' five men that robbed a train down El Paso way. An' here I run onto you fellers. I guess I'm just drawin' to fives these days."

"Yeah?" Charlie Parr inquired sardonically, "An' who was this other five unlucky hombres."

"I might have my suspicions," McLeod told him. "But I never did get to see 'em. If I ever run across 'em I'll know 'em—by their horses' tracks."

"That wouldn't hardly make evidence in court, would it?"

"I don't believe there's a court in this country that wouldn't convict on it—especially if I brought the horses back so that the men who rode on posse with me could see their sign."

"You aimin' to take in five hombres—all by yourself?"

Slag McLeod's face was suddenly grim. "You might as well know, Parr," he said deliberately, "that there hasn't been any five men yet who could bluff me out of an arrest. An' you might as well know, too, that I'm takin' a look at your horses' tracks."

The iron in Charlie Parr's tone matched that of the marshal.

"In that case," he said, his eyes hard, "I better tell you that, speakin' for myself, I never did like the law nosin' around my bronc's tail, an' I haven't seen the star-toter yet that could take me when I didn't want to be took."

For the split part of a second, Lon Carmody thought that Slag McLeod would force the play. Then Doc Grimson spoke quietly. "We're all goin' a little too fast, aren't we?" he asked. "Slag can get a look at our horses' tracks any time he wants to—after we fan the breeze out of town. Until then, I'm afraid he'll just have to exercise that well-known patience of his."

"Patience, hell!" Canuck Bull had come to his senses and was now on his feet. "If you're not out of this town within an hour, you're goin' out feet first. That goes for these two skunks in particular," he indicated Lance and Lockjaw.

Lance Clayton looked at him coldly. "Killin' a United States marshal while resistin' arrest may be murder," he said, "but ventilatin' a swelled-up, over-grown toad frog like you—ain't! Any time you want to go for a gun, go ahead!"

For a brief moment, the boss of Jugtown looked as though he were going to have apoplexy. "I've give you an hour," he growled, turning away. "Better take your chance while you've got it."

CHAPTER 5
GUNSMOKE PLOTTERS

LANCE LOOKED with wonder at the girl walking beside him. He had thought himself in love with more than one pretty girl—in fact, according to Charlie Parr, he fell for every skirt they ran across—but this time it was different. No woman ever had done this to him. She was prettier, he thought, than any girl had a right to be, but at bottom, he knew, it was that voice of hers which got to him. Hearing it in the bank had been impressive enough, but when she spoke to him to thank him for what he had done, he knew then that he was lost. He had insisted on walking back to her restaurant with her.

"You're in danger every minute you stay here," she told him. "Even walking down the street with me, you're in mortal danger."

"I've been in danger ever since I first heard your voice," Lance said. "You're more dangerous to a man than all the bullets in the world."

The girl blushed. It made her look entrancing. "You mustn't say things like that to me," she told him softly.

"I can't any more help it than I can stop my own breathing. I reckon I'll say that to you all the time—whenever I see you."

"Oh!" the girl made a pretty little gesture of despair and distress. "Please! You're not taking it seriously at all. You must! I tell you, it isn't enough to be brave. Canuck Bull is worse than a wounded grizzly—he's not only crazy angry, but he'll be tricky, the way a grizzly isn't. Don't you see what you've done to him?

31

He practically owns this town, and he does run it. He's bullied around here like a king, for years. Now you've knocked him down and bluffed him out of going for you with a gun. He'll kill you for it. He's got to. Unless he kills you, he's done. Don't you see it?"

"Shore sound mighty distressin'," Lance said absently. "What you reckon I'd better do?" His eye had caught the glint of sun on metal from the top of a false-fronted building up the street. The metal had been moving and now there was no more glint.

"He's got enough hired gunmen to kill even the Five Mavericks. He might come out and shoot you down in the open—or he might ambush you. You know, it was just luck that only two of his men were around today. You'd never have gotten out of it the way you did."

"What's he pack this army for?" Lance had noticed that the building up the street was a pretty good place to dry-gulch from. A man could shoot and dart back before anybody got a good look at him. Once in the rear, he could lose himself pretty quickly among the confusion of houses and shacks in the rear.

"Nobody knows," the girl went on. "Nobody asks. It wouldn't be considered—wise. They disappear sometimes and reappear again. That's all I can tell you."

"Um-m." Would the fool shoot while Lance was with the girl? He thought not. A sign down the street read "Jane Venner's Home Restaurant." It was opposite the building with the false front. Lance's unknown friend up there would probably wait until the girl had gone in....

"I declare," the girl at his side said, vexed, "I don't believe you're listening to a word I'm saying."

LANCE SAID hastily, "Yes, I am—wouldn't miss a word for anything. I was just—thinkin'. Who's this jasper that raised your rent that way?"

The girl stopped in her tracks, looking at him in astonishment. "How did you know about that?" she demanded.

Lance saw that he had made a mistake. "Oh, things get around," he covered easily.

"Nobody knows that but me and…" she broke off and then went on, her voice accusing. "You were in the bank when I told that to Lon! That's why he looked so—so upset!"

Lance knew that she had thought "scared" and had not wanted to say it. He did not comment on her accusation. He knew that, after the lead he had given her, it would not be hard for her to figure out what had happened. The Five Mavericks had a reputation which did not exclude robbing banks. Instead he said, "Why doesn't Lon go out gunning for Canuck Bull?"

"I wouldn't want him to," the girl said quickly, defensively.

"Looks to me that wouldn't keep him from it if he wasn't…. I mean if he cared anything about you."

For a second the girl was silent. Then she said, "You musn't think that way about him, too."

Lance asked "Why?" in a voice which had a lot of gentleness in it.

The girl looked up at him helplessly. "Everybody's not—not like—you," she said in a low voice. "Listen—you'll hear it from somebody else, anyway. Lon—Lon Carmody—did go up against

Canuck Bull once." And she told him what had happened. By that time, they had reached the door of the restaurant.

Lance saw that the false front had horizontal cracks in it, where the boards were joined together. One of them was plenty big enough to accommodate the muzzle of a rifle or a six-gun. Through that crack he saw a dark blotch against the sky—a blotch which moved once, slightly. But there was no gun-muzzle pressed against the crack. Apparently the man meant to wait....

"He was only a boy," the girl finished, her voice warm and brooding. "It did something terrible to him, I—nobody understands but—me."

"You—you kind of care a lot about him, don't you?" Lance asked, looking neither at her, nor, apparently, at the false front across the street.

The girl looked at him, her eyes ashamed but honest. "Yes," she said, "I do."

"Aimin' to marry him?" Lance asked, casually.

"I don't think he would marry me now. He's so honest—he knows what has happened to him. And I— Oh! I don't know why I'm talking to *you* about this."

"Even if he was to ask you, you'd wish—well, you'd wish he'd get over it and be a man again, before you married him—is that it?"

The girl's hands were clenched at her side, her face stained with color. "It's so hard to know what to do," she murmured. "Sometimes I think that—that if he wants me, it will help him to be all right again better than if I married him the way he is. He— Oh! I don't know! I don't know!"

Lance's face was without any expression at all. This was the girl he wanted more than he had ever wanted a girl, and she was in love with a yellow skunk…. But how did he know the fellow was a skunk. Maybe, if he hadn't gotten his nerve broken…. There must be something in the fellow for a girl like this to….

"You've made me talk about myself," the girl told him in that voice of hers that made him feel like he was being bathed in warmth. "I meant to thank you. Not many people would have done that—risked everything for a—a stranger."

"I heard your voice," Lance said. "You weren't a stranger any more."

"Please!" the girl said, as though his words hurt her. Then: "Promise me that you'll get out of town right away."

"You don't want to worry about me," he said noncommittally. He thought that she liked him, and that maybe he could make her forget her loyalty to the bank cashier. Then he thought that if she did that, her voice would be a lie. She wouldn't exist any more. That seemed to him the strangest thought he had ever had. It made the world seem mad—and useless.

He put out his left hand, took hers. His right hand was free, but he made up his mind that he would not shoot blind if the muzzle of a gun appeared in the crack. It would be better to duck and run toward the building—get around back and cut the man off.

"I'll always remember you," he said. "Don't wait here with me, I'm just goin' to stand here a little an'—an' think."

"I'll remember you, too—Lance," she said and went into the restaurant.

THE BLOTCH behind the crack moved a little. Lance was staring, apparently, at the ground in front of him, but he saw the gun-muzzle come into the crack, recognized that it was a Winchester.

He wanted to wait the fraction of a second it would take a quick man to sight, so that the man would be sure to squeeze the trigger as he moved. He hadn't often really wanted to kill a man, but he wanted hard to kill the one behind that false front. A killing now answered to some need in him—might still the savage revolt which boiled in him.

His plan of action flashed across the screen of his mind in that fraction of a second between the placing of the gun muzzle against the crack and the instant his tense nerves exploded into action. He jumped forward and sideways, ducking, his hands flashing to his holstered guns.

As he moved there was a report—a report which was somehow double. A bullet whined over his head—not in the least close— and smacked high against the front of the restaurant.

Almost immediately there was a grunt and a scuffling sound from behind the false front. Lance looked up the street to his right. Doc Grimson was standing there, in the middle of the street—a good hundred yards away. A six-gun was in his hand. Behind him were Charlie Parr and Lockjaw and Flint Maddox.

Lance walked across the street, to the rear of the other

building. There was a sawbuck there, and standing on it he could easily reach the low roof. He pulled himself up cautiously. But the man on the roof lay still. When he got to him, Lance saw that he was dead. The bullet had hit him under the shoulder, driving straight through the heart.

Doc Grimson appeared on the roof beside him.

"That was nice shootin', Doc," Lance told him. "I'm obliged."

"It was luck," Doc said. "A Colt isn't that accurate at eighty yards."

The rest of them came up, followed by some curious citizens.

"It's the jasper I punched," said Lockjaw, aggrieved. "How come he wasn't after me?"

The town marshal came up. He had a face like a weasel.

"I've got to put you under arrest for murder," he told Doc Grimson.

He had a gun in his hand and his face was pale. Doc looked at Charlie Parr and they both laughed. Flint Maddox's melancholy vanished in a broad grin.

"You want me to kill him, Doc?" Lockjaw asked belligerently.

The town marshal moved his nervous eyes toward Lockjaw. "I've got the drop on you," he husked. "Don't start anything."

Doc said contemptuously: "Put your gun up, you're not arrestin' anybody. I can draw and put two shots through you before you can pull trigger."

The marshal hesitated, and was lost.

"Put your gun up," Lance told him savagely, "before I twist

your neck. I wanted to kill this dry-gulcher myself, but I'd just as soon polish you off instead."

"You gotta have some respect for the law," the town marshal muttered.

"Leather your iron, Pete." It was Canuck Bull who spoke. He had come up on the roof unnoticed. The marshal put his gun away hastily.

"This fool Horgan had it comin' to him," the big man rumbled. "I give these fellers an hour, an' Canuck Bull keeps his word. If they hadn't of got him, I would have." He turned his back and went over the side of the roof again, without a word or a look to the Five.

Lance Clayton raised his eyebrows. It was evident that Canuck Bull, if he had lost his nerve before, had gotten it back again. It was also plain that he was more of a man than he had appeared to be.

Charlie Parr said irritably, "All right—this is over. Come on—we're makin' pow-wow."

THEY FOLLOWED him. He led them down one of the back streets until he came to a small cantina which looked as though it were for Mexicans. Charlie opened the door, looked the place over, then stepped in.

There was no one else in the place except the fat Mexican behind the bar. They took a table in the corner, with two thick adobe walls at their backs and sat down.

When the Mexican had brought their drinks, Charlie Parr looked at Doc Grimson. "You talk, Doc," he said grimly.

Doc smiled faintly. "Not much need to talk, I reckon," he

said quietly. "The question is, what next? When we leave town we'll have Slag McLeod on our heels. That means a lot of things—hard ridin', for one. A possible killin' for another. If we stay here, we've got to deal with Canuck Bull. I'm told he packs plenty of killers and that he's not a four-flusher. What's your vote, Charlie?"

"I say ride. This bank job's off. I saw McLeod talkin' to that teller. They're goin' to be watchin' us. As for this heap-big bad hombre, Canuck Bull, let him throw his chest around here as much as he wants."

"Aw, shucks, Charlie," Lockjaw said, aggrieved. "I thought we was goin' to rob a bank."

"That's why I want to leave," Charlie snapped. "We'll throw McLeod off the trail, like we did before—then we'll hit the first town that looks likely."

"I kind of hate to go off an' give this tinhorn town-king the idea that he's bluffed us out," Flint Maddox said.

"Why don't we kill him and then leave?" Lockjaw asked hopefully.

"What's your say, Doc?" Charlie asked.

Doc was looking thoughtfully at Lance, who sat brooding, his eyes fixed on the center of the table. "What do *you* think, Lance?" he asked, by way of answer.

Lance shook himself out of his abstraction. "Listen, Charlie," he said, "I'm sorry I messed things up. But the way it is now, I've got a kind of a chore to do around here. You fellers fan the breeze—but I've got to stay."

Charlie groaned. "Lance! Can't you never see a girl without goin' soft on her?"

Lance flushed and looked at the center of the table again. "It ain't that—exactly," he said.

"What's the idea?" Doc asked. "Gunnin' for this Canuck Bull?"

Lance looked uncomfortable. "Not exactly," he said.

"You goin' to stick up the bank, Lance?" Lockjaw asked eagerly.

Charlie Parr cut in ferociously: "Shut up, you blitherin', flop-eared sheep-herder. Ain't we got trouble enough without you askin' fool questions?"

Lockjaw subsided, looking hurt.

"All right," Charlie said resignedly. "We stay. Go ahead, Lance."

Lance protested that he didn't want them or need them.

"All right," Doc said calmly. "You deal it your own way, Lance. But we're stayin' around to see how the game goes."

Lance flushed, shot a grateful glance around the table. "I reckon you've got a right to know," he said. He told them how Canuck Bull had whipped Lon Carmody and what Jane Venner thought about it, then looked embarrassed.

"So we fan lead through Canuck Bull, kill half the town and maybe a federal marshal into the bargain?" said Charlie Parr grumpily.

"No—" Lance said. "We got to keep from killin' Canuck Bull."

"What?" Charlie asked staring. "What you aim to do—make a pet of him?"

"I've got to figure it someway so Lon Carmody downs him," Lance said slowly. "You see, Jane couldn't marry nobody but a *man,* an' she won't marry nobody but Carmody. So, someway, I've got to rig this jasper up so he'll…. I don't see any other way out of it," he ended helplessly.

Doc Grimson reached out and gripped his shoulder. "Old Lance!" he said warmly. "It's an idea, at that."

"You think it can be worked?" Lance asked eagerly.

"Why not? What he needs is nerve. We can put it into him."

"Why, sure," Flint Maddox agreed slowly. "If he had the nerve to go up against him once before—he won't be the first gun-shy hombre that ever got over it."

"I know!" Lockjaw had come out of his sulk and beamed with enthusiasm. "Just as this feller is about to draw against Canuck, I'll shoot him—I mean Canuck. I could be hidin' somewheres…."

Charlie Parr groaned. "Are you gonna shut up or am I gonna shoot you?"

"Aw, shucks, Charlie," Lockjaw protested, not to be robbed of his idea so easily, "you don't see it. You see we could tell this feller that I was goin' to shoot the other one—that way it wouldn't take no nerve for him to go up against him. The way I see, a feller that's yeller ain't no good anyway, so it don't matter if…." He broke off, seeing the tide of crimson that rolled out from behind Charlie's white mustache and surged slowly to the tops of his ears. That was a sign that Charlie was about to lose his temper. Lockjaw relapsed into injured silence.

Lance came to the rescue. "Well, we'll fix up somethin', anyway," he put in hastily. "The first thing is to get in touch with this jasper and see...."

He broke off in his turn, staring. For the door had swung back and Lon Carmody stood on the sill, looking toward them hesitantly.

CHAPTER 6
LESSONS IN LEAD

"**W**HY—HOWDY," LANCE said, recovering a little from his surprise.

"We were just talkin' about you," Doc Grimson said in a quick, cordial voice. "Come in and have a drink."

Carmody came over, looking astonished. "Talkin' about me?" he asked.

Then he apparently thought he understood. He flushed. "I didn't say anythin' to Slag McLeod," he said quickly.

"Hell, that's all right," Charlie said sourly. "We wasn't thinkin' about that. You couldn't prove anythin', anyway."

"We were just saying," Doc put in smoothly, "that we were sorry you had to be the fellow behind the counter there. We'd rather have had you on our side."

Carmody gasped. "You—you'd rather have had *me* on your side?" he asked incredulously.

"Why shore!" Lance said warmly. "That don't surprise you, does it?"

Lon Carmody gulped but found nothing to say. He looked wonderingly from one to the other of the faces before him.

He had come here to ask these men's help. It had taken all his courage to do it. Nothing but his love for Jane Venner could possibly have persuaded him to it. He had meant to confess his own cowardice and helplessness to these men whom he admired more than he had ever admired anybody—and to ask them to do what they could for Jane. And now they were accepting him—the coward, the yellow dog!—as a man like themselves— saying that they'd like to have him on their side! He didn't know what to say.

He took the drink Doc Grimson ordered for him and tossed it off, scarcely aware of what he had done.

It was Doc Grimson, too, who tactfully tided him over the first moments with casual chat about the town and who, when he had finished the second drink, said: "We kind of wondered at a hombre like you working in a bank. It doesn't seem like much for a man of your sort."

Carmody flushed. "I—It isn't much of a job," he stammered. "I—you see…."

He had an impulse to make a clean breast of it then, once and for all, but something restrained him. He couldn't bear just yet to disillusion these heroes of his about himself.

"Sure, we know," Doc Grimson broke in smoothly. "There are times when a fellow's willing to take anything for a while.

But it wasn't hard for us to see that you were another sort at bottom."

Lon wondered if they could have failed to notice how scared he was during the bank hold-up. But already another wonder was beginning to grow in him—a seed merely, the barest sprout—but it was there. If such men as these saw something in him, wasn't there something there?

"I don't see how you could see anything in me," he could not resist saying.

"We think we know something about men," Flint Maddox told him.

"Shore!" Charlie agreed morosely. "We wouldn't get far in our line if we needed a book of explanations with every hombre we run across."

Lockjaw Johnson stared at them wonderingly. "But you just said…" he began.

Charlie Parr glared at him. Lance, with a quick, apparently careless movement, spilled his drink into Lockjaw's lap and then apologized verbosely. Flint stomped on his toe. It was lucky that Lon Carmody was in such a daze. He noticed nothing. Lockjaw shook his head in bewilderment, but he shut up.

"You might be makin' a mistake," Lon said uncomfortably.

"We don't make 'em!" Lance cut in cheerfully. "You were born with guts, feller, an' it sticks out all over you."

This was too much for Lon. He said, "If you knew about the time…."

"We don't need to," Doc Grimson cut him off. "Any man can

The man shot again, and this time the bullet tugged at Lockjaw's shirt.

lose out once. There's plenty of accidents. What counts is what he's made of to begin with."

"Now you take this Canuck Bull," Lance said. "I bet he's a feller that's run it over plenty of jaspers. He's big and strong and fairly good with a gun, so he might have luck for a long time. But the bottom of him's as yeller as a chuckwalla's belly!"

Lon stared. These fellows had just gotten into town. They couldn't have heard anything about him. Yet it sounded almost as though they were talking directly at him. It was a' miracle. Could they be right—about him and Canuck? If he could only find the courage….

Doc Grimson said, "We don't often meet anybody of our kind. How'd you like to ride with us for a while?"

LON CARMODY'S world rocked on its foundations and exploded around him in a blaze of glory. Him? Lon Carmody? Ride with the Five Mavericks? It was like a crowd coming around and telling you you'd just been elected president of the United States. Only Lon wouldn't have felt that that was as great an honor. For a moment, common sense looked through his amazement. There must be something back of this. These men wanted to use him for something, were stringing him along because he might be useful and would throw him over when his usefulness was over. What did they want? Did they want him to help rob the bank?

But that seemed incredible to him as soon as he thought it. Such men as the Five Mavericks did not have to stoop to tricks like that. They could open the Jugtown Bank—or Jugtown itself—as other men might open a tin can. Besides, they weren't that kind. No, there was no other explanation for it. They wanted him—Lon Carmody—because they thought he was a man! They were mistaken, of course. But—*were they?* The question exploded on him in full force this time. Maybe he had just lost his nerve for a little like anybody else might. He had been just a kid. Maybe at bottom he was the kind they thought he was. The idea made his heart swell in him.

"What do you say, fella—are you with us?" Lance asked.

Lon Carmody drew a long breath. Beneath the table his hands clenched into fists. "Am I?" he breathed. *"Am* I? I'll tell a man I am!"

Doc Grimson put out a cordial hand. "I knew it!" he said heartily.

The others followed suit. And then there was a long pause. They looked and felt like men who had bought something and didn't quite know what to do with it.

Charlie Parr broke the silence. "And now what?" he growled, still upset because the bank robbery had fallen through. But despite himself he was warming up to this new recruit to the Bunch. Even with his keen disappointment he was beginning to be curious as to how this would all work out.

"Tell you what we can do," Doc Grimson broke in. "We'll stay under cover until nightfall and then fog it for the Border. We'll hole up there until Lon here has a chance to more or less work into our ways. Then we'll see."

Keeping under cover in Canuck Bull's town was not as easy as it might have been but, with Lon Carmody's help they managed it, and nightfall found them riding hard for Mexico. It was Lon, also, who located Slag McLeod before they started and so gave them so much time that pursuit that night would have been useless.

The Border was not more than an hour's fast ride, and morning found them holed up in the rocky broken country which is the beginning of the Sierra Madre. It wasn't probable that Slag McLeod would follow them into Mexico, but Charlie Parr had taken no chances. He had covered their tracks with every trick he knew.

And that delayed Marshal McLeod—delayed him so that it was two days before he and his posse came to the end of the trail, to the high, rocky plateau where camped the five men he sought, and their new recruit.

DURING THOSE two days a considerable change had come over Lon Carmody. His "training" had begun on the first day.

"Let me see you draw a six-gun," Doc Grimson had suggested.

The others saw that Lon's face went pale. They guessed what was true, that Carmody had not handled a gun since the night of his fight with Canuck Bull—the night Shorty Meldrum had died with a slug in his stomach. Since then the mere sight of a naked gun had made Lon sick. But he said nothing. He had gone home and gotten his old Colt before riding with the Mavericks. Now, he buckled it on wordlessly.

"Go for it when I say 'draw,'" Doc directed.

Carmody stood tense, his eyes nervous. Lance eyed him critically, seeing the stiff position in which he stood, the strain of his muscles.

"Draw!"

The teller's hand jammed down on the butt of his gun, searched a fraction of a second for a firm grip, and yanked the gun out.

Charlie and Lance exchanged significant glances. The draw was so slow he could have been shot several times before his iron cleared. But it was somehow not so slow as they had expected. The worst faults could be corrected.

Charlie looked at Carmody with an artistic expression of surprise.

"Hombre!" he exclaimed. "That's a pretty nice draw you've got there."

Carmody's face went crimson with pleasure. "You think so?" he asked eagerly. Then his face clouded at once. "Canuck Bull can beat that easily," he said.

"Lance can't beat it *easily*," Doc told him, "and you saw Lance beat Canuck."

"I don't mean to say you haven't got any faults," Charlie said, getting really interested, "but the speed's there. When you've got that, the rest is easy."

"Charlie's right," Lance said. "You've got somethin' to learn, but the stuff's there. You'll do."

The others agreed. Lockjaw, who had been taken aside and had it explained to him that Carmody must be encouraged to believe in himself, said, "Hell! He could beat me right now." It was nearly true, but Lockjaw said it with an expression of fatuous complacence which nearly doubled Lance up. Lockjaw could never be brought to believe just how slow his draw was.

Then Doc and Charlie took Lon in hand and began to teach him the things he should know—how to stand relaxed, the muscles of his gun-arm limp, with only the nerves quivering, tense; how to hold his hand, always the same way, so that it met the gun-butt squarely, thumb at the hammer, fingers in place, without fumbling; how to move his hand in that arc which is infinitesimally but vitally shorter than any other possible movement; how to make the muzzle clear leather with the least possible lift—neither to over-draw nor under-draw; and a dozen other fine points in the gunman's economy.

They made him do it by the numbers, slowly, accurately, increasing his speed only when the mechanics of the movement was perfect. They worked him until his gun-arm and his nerves were too tired to respond—then let him rest a while before setting him at it again.

By the end of the first day, they had cut in half the time of his draw. And when they had done that, they looked at one another with hopeless eyes. For trying to teach a man to draw a gun in one day or two is a little like trying to teach a man to fence in an equally short time. The thing requires years to perfect. Years—and tireless, constant practice. Only so, can those infinitesimal parts of a second be slowly rubbed away—the little, dribbling eye-lash flutters which mean the difference between life and death.

Fortunately, the boy was not a bad shot. There was nothing especially remarkable about his shooting, but he could be trusted to hit a man at ten paces, shooting fast from the hip, which was all that was really necessary.

"Gun-fightin'," Charlie Parr told him, now really interested in this making of a man, "is about six parts speed and four parts bluff. If you got the other feller *believin'* you're gonna beat him, he's already half dead. Gents will try anythin' on you, to get you scared of 'em. Pay no attention to it. Be busy tryin' to get them scared of you. When the time comes to draw, forget the other feller's draw. That ain't of no interest to you whatever. If it's faster than yours and he can shoot straight enough, you're goin' to collect some lead. If it ain't, he is. But you can't do nothin' about his draw, so don't even look at it. Think of your own draw and look at the place you're goin' to put your lead. Remember, a gun-fight ain't lost until somebody's dead. Until that's you, you got a chance. If it gets to be you, you won't have to do any worrying about who it is. That ain't one of the worries that dead men have."

"Lead ain't nothin', anyhow," Lockjaw told him patronizingly. "Me, I've had plenty of it. So has the rest of the boys."

Lon Carmody listened. And then, the afternoon of the second day, they arranged a contest for him. He was to try to draw against Charlie Parr. They made the thing look as much like a gun-fight as possible, and when Charlie bellowed, "Fill your hand!" and went for his gun, Lon Carmody made a fairly creditable draw. He could not guess the smooth accuracy with which Charlie, without fumbling or showing any obvious slowness, had gauged his draw so as to beat his opponent by only a shade. It looked real to him, as it would have to any of the uninitiated.

His heart lifted and his eyes blazed in the towering triumph of that moment. It did not matter to him that, even so, Charlie would have killed him. He had drawn nearly even with the old he-wolf himself. That was honor enough for any man to take to the grave with him!

51

Lance Clayton suppressed a smile, but almost immediately sobered down. They were having a lot of success in building Lon Carmody up to where he might have the nerve to go up against Canuck Bull. But—the shrewd realism of Charlie Parr's first comment came heavily home to him now—what were they going to do to keep this boy from being killed? That draw, of which they had made Carmody so fatally proud, might be good enough against the average cow-nurse. But among gunmen…. And Canuck Bull, Lance had seen for himself, was fast—deadly fast—with his Colt.

And, apparently, Charlie Parr was thinking the same thing.

"Yuh learn a lot," he said, "by just thinkin' about it. And it don't wear you down. Think out the whole draw, kid, and first thing you know you'll have it without even liftin' a finger. For instance—" And Charlie went on with his brain practice.

He seemed to have forgotten his bank robbing for the moment. But as Lance watched the oldster he smiled and turned to Doc Grimson.

"Doc," he said, "it looks to me like Charlie's in a hurry to get back to bank robbin'. Seems anxious to learn this kid as much as he can in a big rush. Wants to get it over with."

"Looks like it," Doc agreed.

And then they heard the sudden ring of a rifle shot, the buzz of a vicious bullet crackling high over their heads. United States Marshal Charles Edward—Slag—McLeod, with a brand new posse, was announcing his arrival!

CHAPTER 7
THE STREAK OF YELLOW

THE SHOT came from the rim of the mesa and it was followed by McLeod's voice, "Get 'em high! We've got you covered."

But firing that shot was one of the few bad mistakes in judgment in Marshal McLeod's long and honorable career. It is possible that had he spoken first the Five Mavericks would have thought it wiser to obey. And in any event, his own men would not have been confused as to when to fire. If the Mavericks had moved *after* being warned there would have been no reason to hesitate about cracking down on them. But all five of them were on the ground before the first three words were out of Slag McLeod's mouth.

As a result, the volley which answered their movement was delayed, ragged and inaccurate. Picking a target among that sudden confusion of ducking, rolling figures was difficult, and hitting one of them was like trying to crack down on a sudden covey of fast-flying partridge.

Lon Carmody was the only man on his feet when that volley was fired. He had stood frozen, oblivious to Doc's "Down!" and to the lightning movement of his five companions. Something nipped sharply at his back, and then abruptly, he was on the ground, too.

"Roll! Roll this way!" Lance whispered, urgently. Carmody followed the quick command, and brought up in a shallow wash, with the others.

Lon became aware that his shirt in back was warm and wet and seemed to be burning. He realized that he was hit. The knowledge made him sick at his stomach and he began to shake all over.

"What do you say, Lon?" Doc Grimson asked. "We can stick up a white rag and you can walk out. They can't put you in jail just for having been with us, if you don't help us resist the law."

Lon Carmody wanted badly to take advantage of that opportunity and get out of a situation which promised nothing but disaster, but something in him—perhaps it was merely shame—made him shake his head. "No," he said in a voice which he scarcely recognized as his own. "I'm stickin'."

Doc put a hand on his shoulder. "Good stuff!" he said softly.

THE MESA on which they had been trapped was a small one, roughly a hundred and fifty yards square. It commanded a long view of the country over which pursuit would have to come, so no one had thought it necessary to keep a regular guard. From time to time, every twenty minutes or half an hour, one of them would walk to the edge and look the country over. There had been no sign of anybody. It was evident that Slag McLeod, instead of following their trail directly, had gone around. No doubt he had picked this mesa out as a likely place for them and had crept up on it on the chance. It had been a shrewd bit of work.

The firing had come from two sides—the only two possible approaches, in fact, for the other two sides were abrupt precipices which were virtually unscalable. The shallow wash in which they lay ran from the direction of one of the precipices toward the side which was occupied by the posse. It was really no more than a slight depression and would only give cover to a man lying nearly flat. No doubt it had not been visible from the edges of the mesa, some seventy-five yards away. McLeod must have thought that he had gotten them in the open, without any cover whatever.

To Lon Carmody, when his mind had cleared enough to realize the situation, it seemed that they were just as badly off as though they had no cover. If the posse was bold enough, it could advance at once, as a body, and deliver a deadly fire as soon as the six dared raise their heads. In that case, the fight might be hot for a few seconds but it could have only one end. The attackers would actually have the advantage, and they must number, judging from the sound of that first volley, at least a dozen.

Lon wondered what madness had led him into such a fix. If he had had the faintest sanity or common sense, he thought, he would be safely behind the counter of the Jugtown Bank at this moment, instead of being about to get himself stupidly killed for nothing. After all, he hadn't done anything which made it necessary for him to fight the law. He hadn't done anything to die for. Let these other men die, if they wanted to. It wasn't any business of his. Yet when he thought of telling them so, he could not do it. They had been his idols too long for him to be able to desert them now that they had honored him by taking him along. And maybe it was better to go out with them, gloriously, than to live forever a coward, a mere bank teller, growing stoop-shouldered with the years and the weight of men's contempt.

He didn't know it, but the others were thinking much as he. This was a tight—as tight a tight as they had ever been in. It looked like the end for them, unless they wanted to give up and let Slag McLeod take them to jail. And that, they had no intention whatever of doing. There was no reason, really, why this boy should have to die with them. Yet none of them had the heart to urge him to quit. He had made his choice—the choice any of them would have made in his place—and they couldn't help thinking that he was better off that way. Living the life of a known coward was worse to them than any death could be.

Cautiously, Lon raised his head and looked over his shoulder. The first face that came into his view was Lance's. The sight of it gave him one of the most genuine shocks of his life—a jolt of sheer surprise. The clean-cut, brown, hard-fleshed features were not even pale. There was no change from his ordinary expression, except that his face looked somehow more alive and his snapping blue eyes more intense. Lance Clayton wasn't afraid. He looked as though he was actually enjoying himself!

"Seems to me I remember some mesquite along the edge of this wash," Charlie Parr said, "back toward the other edge. Let's crawl back there, where we'll have some shootin' cover."

Doc Grimson nodded, his extraordinarily luminous gray eyes dancing with some sort of inner intoxication. Lon Carmody did not knew yet that danger—real danger—gave Doc Grimson the same sort of kick that men get out of liquor, but he was beginning to guess it.

"Yeah," Doc Grimson agreed. "We'll have our backs along the cliff that way, too. Maybe we can get a chance to get down it. And if we can't, we can keep anybody else from gettin' up it."

They crawled back. It was painful work and slow. Lon had a feeling that at any minute Slag McLeod would begin his rush— expected to feel a bullet in his back every time he slid another inch forward. The others must be expecting that, too, for every few yards they stopped and appeared to listen. Once Lon thought he heard scraping sounds off to the left, as though the attackers were crawling there, but he could not be sure.

After another few moments, Charlie stopped once more. Lon could hear the sounds this time, more clearly. He became aware that Charlie Parr was looking back at him and winking. Then the oldest of the Mavericks went on. Lon thought that Charlie was acting crazily. The posse'd jump up any moment now and let the Mavericks have it.

HE SAW Charlie had come to the first of the mesquite and had stopped there while Doc Grimson crawled up beside him. They motioned to Lon and the others to stay where they were. Charlie took off his hat and raised his head carefully behind the mesquite. Then he nodded to Doc. Lon saw that their six-guns were in their hands. He remembered suddenly that his own gun was not loaded. He had taken the cartridges out for his practice against Charlie. Now, when he saw the older man raise his guns, he remembered that Charlie's right gun wasn't loaded, either. He had taken his loads out, too. Lon started to tell him.

But before he could speak the guns themselves opened up,

both of them. Besides them Doc's Colts smashed out, rocking, belching pale flame. Lon heard startled cursing to his left, the scrape of running feet, the pound of falling bodies, and a chatter of rifle fire from the mesa edge.

Doc and Charlie were already under cover again, Charlie looking a little grim. At the old timer's gesture, he crawled up to them and the others followed. Lance Clayton wormed past him, seeking the shelter of some mesquite farther ahead. As he passed Charlie Parr he asked: "How many?"

"He sent out half a dozen of 'em, to crawl up on us while the others covered from the rim," Charlie said. "We got three. The others have dug theirselves holes."

"How many at the rim?" Lance asked.

"Six or eight, I reckon."

"Where's this star-toter now?" growled Lockjaw, who also had elbowed his way past Lon.

"He's one of the three that dug in," Charlie said. "Don't kill him, Lockjaw—unless you have to. We shot to disable those fellers."

"I'm plenty tired of that law-hound," Lockjaw said gloomily. "We'd ought to knock him off. What's the use of messin' around with him?"

"You fellers hold 'em here," Lance suggested. "I'm goin' to see what's what at the cliff. Lon, you come with me."

Lon began to crawl again. He was not feeling so much now as though he were going to be sick on the ground in front of him. These men with him weren't quitting—not by a long shot. Something in their confidence and calmness got through to him and slowed up the painful hammering of his pulses. It helped more than he realized to know that the men Doc and Charlie had shot were not dead.

At the cliff's edge, the wash deepened and then ran sharply down to a steep drop in a split in the rocks. Through the split, they could see the basin below where their horses had been turned out, hobbled, to graze. Lon heard Lance curse softly under his breath and then he saw that the horses had been gathered on the other side of the basin and that two mounted men held them by their halters. He noticed, too, that the hobbles had been taken off.

Again, a realization of their situation sent his heart into his boots. He remembered that the saddles and gear were all out on the flat, along with their rifles, in a position which was too exposed for them to get to. And now their horses were in the hands of the posse—well out of pistol range. And the face of the cliff below them was smooth and shelved slightly inward. No man on earth could get down it, unless he dropped a sheer forty feet onto the broken rocks of the base, which spread out in more of a slope but which was itself steep enough. There was nothing to do but stand and fight.

Lance said: "I don't think them fellers have seen us. Get back out of sight."

Lon moved back. "No chance to get down there," he said, surprised at hearing his voice as a sort of croak.

"Not without a rope," Lance said slowly.

"The ropes are all out on the flat," Lon reminded him. "But even if we had one, what good would it do? Those fellers would spot us as soon as we started down and yell to the others. We couldn't cross the basin in time. Besides, all of them jaspers have to do is to fan the breeze with the broncs."

"One thing at a time," Lance said morosely. He was thinking that this hombre was too scared to be any good. It was kind of discouraging to get yourself into a jackpot in order to give another man to the girl you loved, especially when the other man wasn't a man at all, and likely never would be.

After a second, he shook himself and said: "Remember that reata we used to rope your bronc with when he got loose this mornin'? I left it on the edge of the mesa and went down to get some water. It's still there. I'm goin' after it. You stay here an'—an' see that nobody don't find a way up the cliff. If any of the others come up, tell 'em where I've gone."

Lon swallowed hard. "The posse's over there," he got out finally. He looked like he was having trouble to keep from telling Lance that he was crazy. "You can't get the rope from there."

Lance said shortly: "Maybe not. I'm havin' a try at it anyway." HE HAD seen that the edge of the mesa shelved over before the straight fall of the cliff and he guessed that if he kept near the edge, the rise of the ground would conceal him from the view of the posse. There was a good deal of growth, also, near the edge—enough, he thought, to shield him from the eyes of the two men with the horses.

A plan was beginning to form dimly in his mind—a plan which might give them the slimmest of slim chances. But everything hinged on getting the rope.

He crawled out of the wash along the lip of the precipice, and inched his way painfully towards the far edge. The slope there was steep near the corner where the precipice began but got more and more gradual along that side of the mesa. The ground there was rough, broken up by big boulders and some brush. The reata he needed lay about a third of the way from the precipice corner, just where the slope began to ease off.

He reached the edge—to the right of the posse—without being seen and began to make his way carefully over the rough slope which lay between him and his objective. He moved as quickly as possible, yet cautiously.

He had been keeping a big boulder between himself and the posse's position. Now he came up to it and, peered cautiously around. Only one man was in sight. He lay on his stomach with a Winchester in his hands and was not looking in Lance's direction. The rope—Lance could see it now—lay about midway between them, but a little closer to Lance.

Lance eased out from the rock and began to creep forward, one careful step after another. Suddenly he froze, crouching behind a small clump of mesquite which offered him only partial cover. A man had come around the shoulder of ground and had begun to crawl up to take a position at the mesa's edge. He was a big man, with a bull-neck and a face which might have looked plump and jolly had it not been swollen and bruised. Lance's nerves crisped and his pulse beat higher. The man was Canuck Bull, and the course he was taking would bring him very near to the reata!

He had not seen Lance, who was only partially covered by

the mesquite, largely because he was looking at the other man and talking to him.

"McLeod wants to rush 'em," he was saying cynically, "but he's a blame fool. We can wait 'em out until night and then go in on 'em easy. I'm sending Curt into town for more men, but I told Slag we'd try to cover him if he could find anybody fool enough to rush with him. He...."

Bull's hand dislodged a rock and from behind it ran a hideous, long-tailed, sluggish shape which Lance recognized as a chuckwalla. Canuck Bull gave a bellow of fear and jumped to his feet, dropping his rifle and clawing at his six-guns as he stumbled backward down the slope. The other man turned and stared with the same astonishment which Lance felt. The big, harmless lizard was ambling off down the slope, but Bull was not content to let him go. Instead he began to let off his guns, the bullets spatting on the rocks near the lizard but not harming him.

The other man backed hastily away from the mesa rim and moved down the slope to see what was happening.

"What in thunder is it?" he asked. "A rattler? Did he get you?"

Canuck Bull stopped swearing long enough to say: "No! A damn gila monster!"

"A gila! Did he bite you?"

"Naw, I moved just in time! The danged varmint went in under those rocks there. Come an' help me git him."

The other man looked dubious. "Funny place for a gila up here. Sure it wasn't a chuckwalla?"

Canuck Bull looked pugnacious. "I seen it, didn't I?" he asked. "It was a gila monster. Snapped right at my hand, too."

They searched around in the rocks but the chuckwalla had disappeared, and neither of them saw the big-shouldered, lithe-hipped man who flashed out from a low clump of mesquite, snatched up a coiled lariat, and disappeared hastily behind a big boulder.

Lance made his way back over the way he had come, grinning. Canuck had looked plenty funny, stampeded by that fat lizard. He realized that Bull, coming from the north, was familiar neither with gilas nor chuckwallas. The two lizards looked nothing alike to the knowing eye, but for anybody who could not tell them apart, the chuckwalla was, if anything, the more hideous of the two. It was evident that Canuck had a terror of lizards. Men had queer, illogical fears like that. It was dam' funny, though, to see a big brute like Canuck in a panic over anything so harmless as a chuckwalla.

Interesting, too—just as strong men's weaknesses were always interesting, and useful. And had this one been useful!

"So dang scared he couldn't shoot!" Lance thought, chuckling, as he made his way along the lip of the precipice. And right then an idea came to him—an idea which made his heart heavy because he knew it would work.

CHAPTER 8
FROM HELL TO HADES

HE FOUND Lon Carmody still in his place. When Carmody saw the lariat his eyes widened, but he said nothing. He had had time to become thoroughly ashamed of himself during Lance's absence and now that he saw the rope all his old admiration for the Five Mavericks rushed back in full force. These men were hard to beat. If Lance could go over and steal that lariat from under the noses of the enemy, anything was possible. He had heard shooting from that direction and he had wondered whether or not Lance had been killed. The fact that he had let the other go without even offering to do the job himself had added to his shame.

"Crawl back and get the others, Lon," Lance directed him briefly. "Tell 'em all to come here."

When Carmody had started to crawl back Lance busied himself with the problem of trying to find something to tie the rope to. There was nothing. The only thing that looked strong enough to bear the weight of a man was on out-jut of rock a few yards directly below them on the side of the cliff. They could throw a loop over the crag and then swing down on it. But, unfortunately, only one man could get down that way.

The others came crawling up. At the sight of the lariat, Doc Grimson's eyes gleamed. "Great work, Lance!" he exclaimed.

Charlie Parr grinned. "Just in time, too," he remarked. "I think friend Slag is about to start his rush."

Lance explained his difficulty. "Somebody's got to let us tie the rope around his ankle and dig his fingers in to hold us as we go down," he ended. "I'd like to do it, but I think it's pretty near necessary for me to go down first."

"That's my job," said Lockjaw, promptly and with great satisfaction.

"How you goin' to get down yourself?" Lance asked, his eyes twinkling.

Lockjaw looked momentarily taken aback, but he recovered himself quickly. "Don't you worry none about me," he said. "I've fell off of lots higher cliffs than these here. Why up home, we got cliffs that make these here piddlin' little jump-offs look like nothin' at all."

Lance showed him the outcropping. "You can loop that an' swing down. It's a kind of a chance to take, but I don't see any other way out of it."

Lockjaw grabbed the lariat and knotted one end around his ankle.

Lon Carmody's hands began to sweat. The lariat looked tremendously slender, despite the knots which Lance had put in it while he had been waiting for the others. Suppose Slag McLeod came up while a man was hanging to that thing over a forty foot drop to jagged rocks? Suppose Lockjaw got killed and his body slipped down the incline….

Lance dropped the other end of the lariat over the cliff. "All set, big boy?" he asked.

Lockjaw dug his fingers in over a narrow, shallow ridge of rock in the bottom of the wash and grinned. "Go get it, kid."

Lance slid over and dropped from sight.

Lon Carmody saw one of the two men with the horses look up suddenly at the cliff. Lance slid down rapidly, dropped from the end of the rope.

"You next, Carmody," Doc Grimson told him. Lon caught hold of the rope and let himself down. As he did so he saw the man who had looked raise his rifle and begin to shout. A shot cracked into the cliff several yards to his left and below him. He was aware that Lance had whistled, once, shrilly. He slid down the lariat so fast that fine, braided rope ripped the skin from his hands. As he dropped to the rocks below, he was aware of Lance's six-gun blasting the air around his ears. He looked about, saw the big chestnut stallion which he had learned to know as Lance's horse galloping toward them. Lance was cursing and firing his guns frantically.

LANCE CLAYTON had hinged his whole plan on his horse. The stallion, he knew, would come at his whistle. A man holding his halter would have no chance whatever to stop him. The big horse would break free and come running. Once on him, Lance could gallop over to the other mounts, shoot it out with the guards if they resisted, overtake the cavvy if the guards tried to run with them. He would get the horses and bring them back to meet the others. It would be touch and go, for with the shooting in the basin the posse would come up from behind.

Once on the rocks below, however, he hesitated what seemed to him an endless second. He had been a fool to think that the plan would work. What was to keep the guards from shooting, not at him but at the stallion?

He whistled again.

The big chestnut horse flung up a nervous head. Lance whistled again. He could see the stallion jerk sharply on his halter. It came free and the horse lunged into his great, distance-eating gallop. The man who had held him was helpless, his hands full with the other horses. They had become restless and wanted to follow the stallion's example. The other man was already shooting in Lance's direction.

Lance, to make the thing sure, began to shoot his Colt in the direction of the guards, holding high. But the bullets kicked up dust far in advance of his target. Then the man with the rifle took in the situation and snapped a quick shot at the stallion. Lance saw the big horse wince and break his stride, but he did not slacken pace; instead he came on at a dead run. But the guard was not to be robbed of his prey. He steadied himself in the saddle and aimed carefully.

During that instant Lance's heart contracted with agony. The stallion was more than just a good horse to him, more than a chance for his life. He was the horse that Lance loved best in all the world. The great heart of the stallion had carried him a dozen times into and out of danger; had saved his life more than once. Between them was that curious understanding, that great, unspoken loyalty which sometimes exists between a man and his horse.

The man's rifle steadied, lifted a little, steadied again. Lance could almost feel the finger tightening on the trigger. The stallion was going directly away from the rifle. The man could not miss. And then the posseman's rifle jumped and spoke.

Lance saw the white smoke spurt from the barrel, heard the report. But the stallion never wavered.

Bewildered, Lance looked in the direction from which he had thought he had heard another report, saw a drift of smoke from the far hillside. The posseman who held the rifle swayed in his saddle, dropped his Winchester, and then toppled slowly over to the ground. From between two rocks on the hillside a rider on a fiery-looking black horse emerged at a dead run, driving for the other guard and the horses.

The remaining guard dropped the halter ropes and started to run, but after an instant he appeared to see that the man who charged toward him was alone. He pulled up and clawed for his six-guns. The other came on, riding hard. When he was within Colt-range the guard fired, once. The rider on the black horse had shot also, and more accurately. The posseman joined his partner on the ground.

The stallion thundered up to Lance, and slid to a stand-still whinnying. Lance leapt for his back, turned him toward the cavvy.

They had scattered, scared by the shots, but Lance saw that the rider on the black horse was after them, his lariat sailing at the leader. And then he saw something else—something that lifted his heart like a familiar song. The rider on the black horse was Don Ricardo Perez y Gonzales, sometimes known as Ricky—smuggler and friend!

BACK AT the cliff things had been happening with the same rapidity and suddenness with which they had happened in front of Lance. The horse-guard's shouts had been too faint to understand and the crack of his rifle had, it appeared, merely caused Slag McLeod to hesitate a moment longer. But as Lance's six-gun began to bark below, the rush began. When no shots came to greet them from the mesquite, Marshal McLeod evidently guessed the situation. He yelled, "They've gotten down! You fellers on the rim, go after 'em. Come on, boys, we'll pick 'em off from the cliff."

He counted without Lockjaw Johnson.

Lockjaw had said: "Git over, two at a time. The rope'll stand it."

Charlie Parr had piled over after Lou Carmody, and the instant that Carmody hit the ground Flint was on the rope Doc Grimson, who had arranged that order, dropped over next. As he did so, he heard Slag McLeod yelling orders, but he was three yards down before he felt a heave on the rope and made up his mind that he had to go back. He remembered that Lockjaw had to draw the rope up, disengage his ankle, make a loop, and snare the outcropping before he could drop down. If McLeod and his men were racing across the flat Lockjaw wouldn't have time.

Not that the heave on the rope was a signal to Doc. It just happened to coincide with his thinking. Also, he noticed, it lifted him half a yard nearer the top. Climbing hand-over-hand up a slender lariat is no easy job, but Doc's steel-like, supple muscles made a quick job of it. He was already reaching for the ledge of the rock when Lockjaw's six-gun roared.

Lockjaw had heard McLeod's shouted order and the pound of running feet and he had smiled with satisfaction. With two men still on the reata he had dug his ham-like hands in and hitched his big frame forward, the muscles in his neck and back standing out like steel cables. By a tremendous effort he had gotten one knee under him and heaved forward again. In the middle of that heave, Flint had dropped off the end of the rope and Lockjaw went face forward into the bank of the wash. He hitched himself forward again, however, and that heave brought him to where he could see the level ground of the mesa and the men, half a dozen of them, racing towards him.

He reached for his Colt and leveled it at the running form of Slag McLeod. His big hand steadied, rock-like, and the Colt bellowed its welcome to the posse. Slag McLeod went down heavily, with a bullet through his thigh.

Lockjaw thought: "Charlie ought to have let me kill him," regretfully, then turned his gun on the next of the attackers. The possemen were firing now, however. Bullets swarmed around Lockjaw's head. One drew a spurt of blood from his cheek. Another kicked dirt into his eyes and caused him to miss his second shot. Lockjaw swore disgustedly and aimed again at the same man. As he did so, Slag McLeod raised one of his guns and leveled it at Lockjaw's head.

It is probable that the big, barrel-chested Maverick would have died then, had it not been for a curious accident. Slag McLeod, who had the reputation of never missing, missed. When he fell, wounded in the thigh by Lockjaw's first shot, his right gun had ploughed in the dust, collecting enough dirt to clog the barrel. When Slag shot, the barrel split and the gun jumped from his hand.

Lockjaw's shot did not miss. The man he aimed at clutched at a smashed shoulder and sat down suddenly. Then Doc Grimson's Colts were barking at Lockjaw's side. Slag McLeod's second gun flew from his hand, shot out of his grasp by one of Doc's unerring bullets. A third man dropped, shot in the hip. The other three dived for the cover of the same wash which sheltered Doc and Lockjaw. The twisting course of the wash protected them from further fire but it also protected the two Mavericks from them.

Doc motioned to Lockjaw and took to the reata again. He went down fast, and three seconds after he had disappeared over the edge, Lockjaw was pulling the lariat up and running it through the hondo. One throw did the work. The rope settled about the outcropping.

Lockjaw drew it fast and swung down. He might easily have held his breath as he did so, for the lariat was none too secure around the outcropping, but Lockjaw had probably never held his breath in his life. He swung down hard, driven by his big weight, and swung out in a pendulum-like arc down under the outcropping then back scraping against the side of the cliff. At the same time, something else smashed against the cliff near him, with a vicious spat. He realized that it was a bullet.

The man shot again and this time he was close. Lockjaw felt the bullet tug at his shirt. "You skunk!" he bellowed, furiously. "Wait until I get down from here and I'll take you apart."

He began to slide down the swinging rope, not half so much to escape the third shot which the posseman was aiming at him as to make good his threat.

71

CANUCK BULL and the rest of the covering party had not been slow to respond to the excitement below. At the guard's first shot, Bull himself had slipped down from the rim, guessing that the men they were after were managing to get down the cliff. The rest had remained at their posts until McLeod's shout had released them, then they too had gone plunging down the slope and raced around toward the basin.

Lon Carmody, on his feet beside Lance, had responded to the marshal's shout in a way which would have surprised himself had he not been acting practically automatically. The warning shout had told him that danger would come from the corner at the end of the cliff. "Somebody's got to keep 'em off," he thought excitedly, and found himself running in that direction.

He went a long way—almost to the corner of the mesa—before he met anybody. Then a man came plunging around the comer and Lon flung up his Colt to fire. In that instant, he realized two things, one was that the man before him was Canuck Bull. The other was that his gun was empty!

He had not reloaded back there in the wash when he had first remembered that he and Charlie had emptied their guns to draw against one another. He had been ashamed to let the others see him do it after he understood that Charlie had already done so long before.

Now, for the second time in his life, he was helpless before Canuck Bull's six-gun, and that six-gun was trained squarely on him. Then, to his infinite amazement, Canuck Bull dropped his gun without firing and plunged forward on his face. At the same instant, Lon was aware that a Colt had spoken behind him.

He turned and saw Charlie Parr behind him, a trickle of smoke oozing from the muzzle of one of his ancient hawglegs. Charlie was a long distance away, and Lon found it hard to believe that it was he who had shot Canuck Bull. But there was no one else who could have done it.

Two other men came plunging around the corner and Lon flung himself down behind a rock and began to jam shells into the cylinder of his gun.

Lon could hear shooting up on top of the mesa now. Lockjaw wasn't down and neither was Doc Grimson. He wondered if they were in trouble. Two more men came around the corner, and Lon began to shoot at them.

He missed twice before the men dodged back out of sight. Dimly he was aware that somebody behind him had also fired and he saw that his hand was shaking badly. It scared him to see that, for he knew that he had missed twice because of it and it came to him that even if his gun had been loaded he would have missed Canuck Bull and been killed if Charlie hadn't been handy. But somehow the fear angered him and that anger steadied him.

One of the men in front of him stuck a cautious head and gun-hand around a rock. Lon flung a shot at him and saw the rock chip off in front of his face. The head disappeared suddenly, and Lon knew that if he had had the whole face to shoot at, he would have hit it almost squarely. What he did not know was that his shot had missed wide. Charlie Parr's slug, the report of which had been drowned in the roar of Lon's own gun, had chipped that rock. And Charlie, so far from congratulating himself on coming so close, was swearing viciously at having missed. That was the third shot he had missed in rapid succession. It was true that Canuck Bull had fallen, evidently hit in the head, but Charlie had shot for the center of his face which was the only target he had, and he had seen no sign of the bullet landing there.

Lon, however, had begun to get some confidence in himself. He wished that Canuck Bull hadn't been killed. He'd like to try a shoot-out with him right now. And with that thought came the realization that Bull's death was, for him, Lon Carmody, an irreparable tragedy. Never any more could he even hope to make up for the cowardice he had shown before Canuck. In a flash of insight, he realized that he had always held the dream that some day he might really redeem himself by facing the terrible Bull again. It had been, without his knowing it, the thing that had kept him alive and in Jugtown. Even more than his hopeless love for Jane Venner had been the possibility of regaining his own self-respect. And now Canuck Bull was dead and Lon Carmody was a lost soul.

Rage swelled up in him—rage against himself and the fate which had played him such a scurvy trick—rage and self-disgust and despair. Then he heard a shot in front of him. He could not see the man who fired and wondered what he could be shooting at. Another shot followed close on the heels of the first one, and Lockjaw's furious bellow burst on his ears. It came to him that the man in front of him was pot-shooting at Lockjaw, who was helpless to shoot back, and at the same moment he saw Charlie Parr running forward, a gun in each hand and his eyes blazing. And this time, Charlie was not trying to take advantage of cover.

Lon also jumped to his feet and leaped for the rock which sheltered the hidden marksman. He was mad clear through now. The soreness of sitting there doing nothing while a man shot twice at one of his partners was added to the rage he felt against himself for having waited too long to get Canuck Bull. He jumped straight for the rock, careless of how much noise he made. The man must have heard him coming, for when he came in sight of him the fellow was crouched there waiting, his eyes flaring a sort of defiant fright. They fired together. Lon felt the breath of a bullet hurtling past his cheek and then saw the other man double up.

He was to learn later that his bullet had ricochetted from a heavy metal belt buckle which the posseman wore. The shock of the blow had knocked him out—otherwise he was unhurt. But Lon believed that he had killed him and, while it made him feel a little sick, it raised in him, too, an overwhelming pride. For he had recognized the man as one of Canuck Bull's henchmen and a known gunman.

CHAPTER 9
DEATH SITS LIKE A BUZZARD

H E FELT a touch on his arm. Charlie Parr had come
up. "Nice work," the old timer said gruffly. "Come on.
We're fogging it."

Together they ran back to the others. Lon saw that all the
horses were there and that a Mexican-looking man on a fiery
black horse had unaccountably appeared from somewhere. The
next moment he was mounted, bare-back, and they were off at
a full gallop. Bullets whistled past their heads, but nobody was
hit, and in a matter of seconds they were out of range.

A minute's hard riding brought them over a rise and out of
sight even of the mesa top. Ricardo, who was in the lead with
Lance, pulled his horse down.

"Listen, amigo," Charlie Parr spoke gruffly. "We better make
some time. There's a gent back there that don't know the meanin'
of the word quit. He'll be on our trail pronto."

Ricardo smiled. "You are talking about the good Marshal
McLeod—no? You are right, my fran'. He ees the devil himself,
that man. Me, I am more scare of this McLeod than I am of
my future life, which ees bad—ver' bad. But here, we are in my
contry—yess! I theenk that pretty soon we weel ride away—ver'
far away—from thees Marshal McLeod."

"You can trust to this hairpin, Charlie," Lance said. "He's a
crazy Spick but he knows every crooked trail in this country
like I do the shape of a corkscrew."

"Cr-razy Spick!" retorted Ricardo scornfully. "Am cr-razy,

yes—loco—because I am not having sense enough to choose the right kind of fran's. But I do not get myself in big tro'ble biccause I weesh to save the pretty ladies from these so bad hombres—no!"

Charlie Parr grunted. Lance shot him a covert glance and suppressed a grin. He knew Charlie had been working himself up to a peeve for a long time, ever since Lance had walked out and spoiled the bank robbery. But he knew also that Charlie had to pretend to be sore even to himself.

Charlie would have done the same thing. In his heart, Charlie was as soft as warm butter. But he had once given up the leadership of Boot Hill Kennedy's gang because a bank cashier's pretty wife had walked in on a hold-up and put her soft young arms in front of the safe and said she would die before she let anyone rob it—he had fiercely forbidden his men to lay a hand on her—and now he had to pretend to be tough, somehow.

Lance said to Ricardo. "Sh! Don't talk about it. Charlie Parr's already after my scalp for that. He's in favor of insultin' young girls. He's plenty bad, Charlie is—a cultus bad hombre!"

Charlie said sourly: "I'm bad enough to want to make some profit out of riskin' my hide, without some young romantic idjit string-haltin' the play every time a pretty gal comes over the skyline."

Lance looked at Doc and caught cold devils dancing in his eyes. "Did I understand you to say that your friend could lead us most anywhere we wanted to go, Lance?" he asked.

"Shore! And then some," Lance told him.

"Then maybe he could lead us back to Jugtown," Doc suggested.

Charlie Parr stared at him. "Doc, you ain't gone loco too, have you?" he inquired, aggrieved.

"Well," Doc said reflectively. "I been thinkin' about this Canuck Bull. He was mighty active in that posse. That seems plumb sinful to me—and I hear he runs a pretty warm gambling house. This is Saturday night. If we were to step in and lift the big money off the tables I bet this Bull would be plenty irritated."

Charlie's eyes widened, then his wrinkled face broke into a grin. "Doc," he said. "There's times when I under-rate you, an' them times I'm most gen'rally sorry the very next minute."

Flint's melancholy, which had settled on him the moment the excitement of the fight had died down, lifted. "It's a plumb fine idea, Doc," he said. "Beats robbin' the bank all holler." Flint did not like robbing banks and risking the chance of causing ordinary hard-working folk to lose money.

Ricardo lifted his hat with a flourish, "Amigo," he said gravely to Doc Grimson, "I salute you."

"But Canuck Bull's dead," Lon Carmody said. "Charlie Parr shot him."

Doc Grimson shook his head. "I'm afraid Charlie didn't do a good job, Lon," he said. "I saw Canuck Bull, or his ghost, shooting at us as we rode away."

Charlie Parr slapped his thigh disgustedly. "Creased him!" he exclaimed. "Dang it, I'm gittin' old! I'm slippin'!"

Lon Carmody was speechless. Half of him felt like a man

reprieved from a life sentence; the other half felt like one condemned to be hanged. Canuck Bull was alive. Nothing was changed!

"Anyway, Ricky's not slippin'," Lance put in. "He didn't do any creasin' of the feller that was goin' to shoot Tomahawk, here. How'd you happen to show up just at the right minute, Ricky?"

"I have heard those things which happen in Jogtown—no? I theenk, these amigos of mine have make themselves some tro'ble. That ees ver' bad tro'ble when Señor McLeod look at your tracks and say: 'I want these men.' I see heem when he come to look for a posse. Our fran', Canuck Bull, he offer heemself an' hees men. He say you have stayed in Jogtown longer as the hour he geeve you so you mus' be keel. Señor McLeod say 'no,' he weel take you to jail, bot El Toro say you weel fight, so he have to keel you anyhow. He come weeth hees gunmen. When Señor McLeod sees hees posse he look a leetle seeck. Me, I see that he theenk, 'more better eef I go after these *perros* weeth the Mavericks than to go after the Mavericks with soch boms.' Bot he shrog hees shoulder an' they go off. Me, I am following along a leetle. I theenk, maybe I fin' them firs', then I make the so small whisper in their ear—no?

"Bot eet could not be thees way. I am not finding you firs'. So—I do what I can—no?" Ricardo shrugged with the fatalistic air of one who excuses himself for something which is not his fault.

"Boy," said Lance admiringly, "You did what you could an' it was plenty!"

The Mexican smiled and made a little gesture of deprecation.

"It is nothing. I do myself one leetle favor, also. You remember the other night? I don' see those men ver' good, but I have ver' good ear for the voice. One man, he speak to you—no? I remember that voice. Also I have see something shining on the hat of thees man. It is something—some silver, I theenk—ver' high on the crown of hees hat. Not many people wear the silver up there. Today, when that man see you, he holler—no? Also I see one thing shining on hees hat. I weel shoot to save your horse, yes—but I weel maybe shoot hees horse instead, to spoil hees aim—no? Only I remember that voice and that piece of silver so—I don' shoot the horse."

"No," Doc said thoughtfully. "You didn't shoot his horse. I wonder—I wonder if your friend Canuck Bull was at the bottom of that little fracas you had the other night."

Ricardo flashed him his sudden grin. "I have heard some leetle theengs," he answered. "One or two, only. I theenk maybe you have guessed right. I theenk maybe eet ees not enough for Señor Bull to have the gambling house an' the silver mine an' the bank. I theenk he mus' have a leetle what you call smoggling also."

HE HAD been leading through a twisting maze of arroyos and ravines. Now he turned suddenly up a rocky slope, plunged down into a hidden canyon which ran, narrow and twisting, angling back toward the direction from which they had come. The floor of the canyon was sand-covered. At one point a steep path led up to a high chimney-rock which thrust up from the rim of the canyon walls. Ricardo halted them and drove his black pony scrambling up the path. At the rim of the canyon, he left the horse and went on foot up the rock. A few seconds later he came down again.

"He ees make a mistake, el Señor McLeod," he grinned. "I theenk now we walk a leetle."

"What I can't make out," Flint Maddox said thoughtfully, "is how come Slag didn't try to round us up in Jugtown. He must have follered us there."

"No! No!" Ricardo assured him. "I have heard. That one was leetle what you call accident. He lost you. Then he come to Jogtown biccause that ees where he work now. He ees to stop the smoggling there. Ver' many Chinamen an' Mexicans an' opium are crossing the Border. The gove'ment do not like that. McLeod he has been working on that. Me, I am moch afraid. But behol'! The first thing he see, ees the Five Mavericks! Som' surprise, eh?"

"It'll be one on Slag if his posse turns out to be the smugglers he's after, won't it?" Charlie Parr grinned. "I tell you what—this Canuck Bull looks like the right sort of meat to me. When we're through with his gamblin' house, we'll take his bank. By Dad! I started out to stick up a bank an' I ain't goin' to be happy until it's done!"

Lockjaw beamed with joy, but Flint and the others looked doubtful.

"If we do that," Flint objected, "it'll look mighty bad for Lon, here. He was seen with us an' they'll say it was him that give us the lay of the bank."

"I guess it don't matter much," Lon said soberly. "I'm outside the law anyhow, now."

He was thinking about the posseman he thought he had killed that afternoon. The man had been sworn in as a temporary federal deputy. Killing him amounted to murder. From now on, Lon Carmody would be a wanted man. But somehow the thought did not depress him much. He had too much pride because he had actually faced somebody in a gun-fight and come out on top. And besides, wasn't he a member of the most famous band of outlaws in the country—he, Lon Carmody, the one-time yellow bank clerk?

Lockjaw spoke slowly, like a man who has finally fought his way to a conclusion. "Lon," said, looking immensely awkward and somewhat ashamed. "I got to tell you that I haven't been thinkin' much of you. Ever since the boys told me you was… er…." He hesitated, catching the quick flash of warning in Lance's eyes. "Anyways," he concluded, "I got to hand it to you for the way you went after that jasper that was tryin' to down me. Not," he added hastily, "but what I wouldn't have got him. But you done your part." He stuck out his ham-like right hand. "What about shakin' on it?"

Lon flushed and put out his hand. Something told him that Lockjaw had been about to say something he wouldn't have liked to hear, but that was nothing to him beside the fact that the barrel-chested Maverick had really wanted to shake his hand.

"I saw that as we rode up, Lon," Lance told him. "It was a mighty nervy play you pulled there."

The others joined in then. And before they got through Lon Carmody was feeling that being outside the law was a small price to pay for the approval he was getting. After years of scorn, and self-hate, it was like strong liquor to him.

But Lance, riding ahead with Ricky, appeared sunk in gloom. His plan for helping Carmody had gone plenty sour. It was true that the fellow showed some signs of being a man, after all. It might even be possible to get him to go up against Canuck Bull, and help him to win. But Carmody, as a wanted man, was as far from being able to make Jane Venner happy as ever. All the Mavericks had done was to enable him to jump from the frying pan into the fire.

Ricardo looked at him out of the corner of his eye. "Why you do it, *nino?*" he asked. "Why you don't take her for yourself?"

Lance looked at him in astonishment. "What do you know about it?" he asked.

Ricky shrugged, and said in Spanish. "I didn't ride with you so long without learning something about you. Someone whispered to me that you knocked Canuck Bull down for a señorita and that you walked with her afterward. Me, I have seen this señorita. I have heard her speak. Ah, that voice! I know what that did to you. And then I hear that you have taken the bank teller with you. All the world knows that story, my friend. Now, I see you sad. I put two and two together. It is simple, no?"

Lance said simply, "We've ruined it now. He's goin' to be on the dodge, from now on."

Ricky spread his hands in a gesture of indifference. "So much the better. Take her for yourself. Me, she will not look at me. If she did, how quickly I would run with her. Not even you could stop me, amigo."

Lance shook his head. "Make her the wife of an outlaw?" he asked. "Besides, she's sweet on him."

"De nada!" Ricky said impatiently. "They change, these little pigeons. Also, the law is nothing to them."

Lance did not answer. An idea was beginning to take shape in his mind. Presently, he looked up, his eyes flashing.

"Look here, Ricky," he said eagerly. "If Canuck Bull is in this smuggling, that whole gang of his may be in it, too."

"I think so, yes."

"Then if we could prove it, what Lon did wouldn't be a crime. If we could turn the proof and the whole crowd over to Slag McLeod, we could explain that Lon was just helping us to run 'em down and that they knew it. He had to keep from bein' taken, so as to get the deadwood on them and also because they'd have ventilated him if they'd gotten their hands on him."

"You think Señor McLeod would believe that?"

"Maybe not, but he'd pretend to. He's not a bad hombre, McLeod. He'd give Lon his chance."

Ricky reached out a hand and put it on Lance's shoulder. *"Nino,"* he said softly, "I think you are a big fool but I think also that you are the whitest fool I ever knew. You know that I will help you in your folly, don't you?"

"Thanks, pardner," Lance said. His voice sounded a little heavy.

They rode in silence a little and then Ricky said: "I think the mine is the place to look. It is so well guarded, that mine, yet it is only a silver mine. I have seen some of the ore, and it does not seem to me so rich. I think if I had that mine I would not guard it so much."

Lance looked at him. "Then if a feller could get up to the mine..." he said softly.

Ricky nodded. "But it will not be easy, my friend," he warned. "Death sits there like a buzzard, waiting."

Lance said nothing, but his jaw was set.

Ricky sighed. "Yes," he said in English, "he ees cr-razy, thees Spick."

CHAPTER 10
HOT LEAD GIFT

THAT NIGHT the Jugtown Palace Saloon and Gambling Parlor was in full blast. Customers lined the bar, and flocked in groups to the tables where the spinning click of roulette wheel mingled with the rattle of ivories and the low-toned, even voices of the men who dealt faro and monte. It was a rough crowd, drawn about equally from the nearby mines, the neighboring cattle ranches and the riff-raff which drifted in and out across the Border, bent on various and mysterious business.

It was not the kind of crowd that most riders of the Owlhoot Trail would have picked to stick up. There were too many fast guns there, too many reckless faces, too much chance for somebody in some corner to start the fireworks. And if that gang once got its shooting irons unlimbered, it would be just too bad for whoever was trying to rod the hold-up.

Something of all that was in Lon Carmody's mind as the gang stopped outside that night and began to get out of their saddle bags the worn, non-descript coveralls and the battered sombreros which had served so often to conceal distinguishing marks of identity and make it difficult for witnesses to a hold-up to positively identify the men under them. Lon himself was dressed in ordinary range clothes—the clothes he had once worn as a puncher and which he had not donned in so long that they would be as effective a disguise as any.

Doc's plan was to leave him, with Flint, outside as lookout. But after some thought and a struggle with himself Lon had asked to be allowed to go in with the others, and Lance, who knew what Carmody was feeling, had put in a word for him.

"All right," Doc had assented, disregarding Charlie's sour look, "but remember, don't do any shooting unless you absolutely have to."

All of them knew that it was a dangerous thing to do. Fear did curious things to men—sometimes it made killers of them. In any case, it took good nerves for the kind of work the Mavericks did. A nervous and inexperienced man might do all sorts of harm. But they had set out to make a man of Lon Carmody and Doc felt that they had to take the risks involved.

They came into town by a back way and dismounted, quietly, not behind the Jugtown Palace but behind the darkened building across the way. Doc Grimson, unmasked, strolled quietly to the front, then at his signal the others came quickly. No one was in the street near them. At the front door of the saloon, they paused the fraction of a second to adjust their bandanna masks, then Doc Grimson led the way through the door.

Lon Carmody, by arrangement, was last. He saw Doc, Lance, and Charlie go through the door, fast, with Lockjaw following at his awkward, lumbering gait. Before Lon could get into the saloon he heard Doc's voice, crisp, commanding, with an edge of danger in it, "Elevate 'em, gents. This is a stick-up."

As Lon came in, blinking a little against the light, he saw that the first three had moved quickly to commanding positions, where they could best cover all angles of the room. Lockjaw was still at the doorway, his posture, even the set of the two Colts in his big hand, belligerent, menacing. But what impressed Lon most was the deadly steadiness of those guns, not just Lockjaw's but those of all the rest. His own heart was pounding wildly with excitement and his gun-hand shook slightly as he fought fiercely against it. That scared him even more than the fact that he was taking part in his first robbery. He was letting the others down. The crowd would see that trembling hand and someone would make a break for his gun. He set his teeth and lowered his Colt until it hung at his side, pressing it against the flap of his chaps.

"Back up against the walls, gents," Doc said coldly. "We're not robbing any of you and we're leavin' the money that's on the tables where it is. All we're taking is the house-money. So none of you's got any call to get yourself killed. Move lively now—and don't make any foolish plays."

The crowd, its hands up, began to move back toward the

walls. Then it happened. One of the house dealers evidently thought he saw his chance. His hand flashed to the shoulder gun under his coat and came out fast. Lon Carmody saw it and—stood frozen. Then a Colt roared, deafeningly. The gambler gave a shocked gasp and staggered, his gun arm falling limply to his side, the weapon dropping to the floor.

Doc Grimson's voice cut sharp across the echoing silence which followed the shot. "Hold it, everybody! Nobody's going to get hurt who doesn't move. But the next man who tries anything is going to get hurt worse."

Lon saw that it was not Doc's gun which was smoking, but Lance Clayton's. He saw, too, that the gambler must have had his shoulder smashed, because he had clutched at it and then sunk into a chair, moaning.

The shock of the shot and the sight of a man hurt and moaning had almost smashed Lon's nerve. He shook all over and wished to God he had never turned outlaw, and wondered if he was going to be sick, there in view of everybody.

The crowd gave back. Nobody reached for a gun again. One lesson had been enough even for this hard-boiled crew. Lon saw that Charlie Parr was herding the men who had been at the bar, including the two bartenders, over with the others. As the crowd shifted its position the Mavericks shifted with it, silently, like a well-oiled machine. Everybody was covered every second of the time.

In the movement, Lance Clayton passed close to Lon. "Steady, kid," he said in a low tone, "this is goin' to be easy."

His voice was casual, with an almost cheerful note in it—and it was friendly. Shame flooded up in Lon and suddenly he felt steady—rock-steady. He shifted with the others, picking out the second which seemed to him the least guarded and casually raised his gun. His hand no longer trembled.

DOC GRIMSON bolstered his guns and stepped toward the vacant tables. Calmly, methodically, with sure, quick movements, he scooped up the bills and gold and silver which stood before the dealers' places. True to his promise, he left the money which had been put down as bets.

The door opened and two men came in. They had their hands over their heads and behind them was Flint Maddox, masked with a gun in each hand.

"Couple of sight-seers," he announced briefly. "An' somebody's comin'—horseback and fast. About half a dozen, from the sound."

Lon saw that none of the others had turned their heads at the sound of the entrance. Charlie Parr was placed back, so that he had the door covered. That was enough for the others. He blushed under his mask to think that he himself had turned. During that instant, the men in front of him might have drawn.

Charlie Parr said to the two men: "Git over against the wall, pilgrims." Then to Flint: "All right, we're about through."

Flint stepped out through the door again.

Doc Grimson gathered up the last of the visible cash on the tables and then went to the till behind the bar.

Flint reappeared. As he did so, Lon could hear the noise of hearses sliding to a halt outside while men dismounted.

Flint said: "McLeod and his gang," crisply.

Doc Grimson said, "We'll go out the back door, boys. Get goin'."

He took the money out of the till and stuffed it unhurriedly into his bulging pockets.

Lon saw that the others were backing toward the rear of the building, still keeping the crowd covered. He did likewise. His pulses had begun to pound again, but his hand was still steady enough.

Then the front door swung open and Canuck Bull stood there, his mouth falling open. But his hands drove for his guns. Doc Grimson's Colts thundered twice. Instantly, there was darkness, with the tinkle of broken glass falling from the ceiling lights.

Lon turned stumbling towards the door, ran into the wall. The room began to fill with the roar of guns and stabs of flame. Lead smacked into the wall behind him. Somebody caught him by the elbow and pushed him through the door. Then they were running through the darkness outside. He could hear yelling and confusion in the saloon behind them.

Doc Grimson led the way around a corner of the building and straight for the main street. Lon thought that was madness. There would be somebody there, surely, and they would have to pass the wide, lighted street under the guns of the men who would come swarming out of the saloon. But he followed in silence.

When they got to the street he saw that he was wrong. People were piling out of other saloons and beginning to appear in windows and doorways but nobody had come out of the Palace.

He realized that nobody could come out of the Palace, with the posse piling through the door at Canuck Bull's yell. And the other people would not know enough to shoot at them.

But they had counted without Slag McLeod. The marshal had been immediately behind Canuck Bull and had seen Doc Grimson shoot out the lights. Somebody had yelled: "They're going out the back!" and Slag had not wasted an instant. It would have been foolhardy to run through that saloon, with the guns blazing in it, so he turned and darted out the front door. Luck had it that he dashed first to the wrong corner of the building, but luck had it also that his quick ears caught the pound of the Mavericks' feet as they raced along the other side.

He brought up sharp and whirled, guns ready. As the six figures raced out into the light, the guns came up—steadied. "Halt!" he yelled, "in the name of the law."

Every one of the Five Mavericks guessed who had shouted that. There wasn't another man in Jugtown, probably, who would have given them that chance. And not one of them but realized that the showdown had come. They were not a quarter of the way across the lighted street. And at that range, guns like Slag's could not miss.

It was time to shoot it out with Marshal Slag McLeod!

Doc Grimson brought up short, whirling. "I'm takin' him," he called sharply, "stay out of it! I'm gettin' you, Slag," he snapped, and his hands drove for his guns.

Those who watched that night saw a draw then such as they had never dreamed was possible—the flashing, magic draw of Doc Grimson at his best. The Colts seemed to leap, too fast to be seen, from their holsters. Men swore that they had come into his hands from out of the air, hammers thumbed back, ready-leveled. But the draw could never have been fast enough. Not with those guns of Slag McLeod's already leveled and ready.

Then something happened then which nobody expected. A Mexican had been lounging all the while in front of the Palace Saloon. He had drawn back into the shadows when the posse arrived, but he had emerged an instant later. He was a slender, handsome-looking figure, flashily dressed, and the smile with which he had greeted the arrival of Canuck Bull and McLeod had been flashy, too—sudden brilliant gleam of white teeth under the short black mustache.

He had been lolling lazily but with a curious air of nonchalance and gallantry about him, and when McLeod had stopped with ready guns to let the Mavericks come out into the open, the Mexican had strolled toward him carelessly. Now, however, as Doc called his challenge, the leisurely figure galvanized into life, moving like a flash. He leaped for McLeod, pouncing on him from the side and behind, cat-like. As the hurtling figure drove into him, the marshal's guns exploded, the shots going wild. Doc Grimson's guns were never fired. His thumbs caught and pressed back the hammers in the very instant of letting them go.

"Run!" he snapped at the others, and set the example himself. Men boiled out of the door of the Palace, guns blazing. But the first bullets were too fast and wild, the second burst too late. The six robbers disappeared into the darkness between two buildings and a second later Jugtown heard the pound of hoofs that raced away into the night.

IN FRONT of the Palace Slag McLeod struggled savagely free, flinging a lithe, flashily-clad figure from him. Ricardo Perez y Gonzales fell heavily, lay relaxed, a slow stain starting from his shoulder.

"Dam' you," Slag McLeod snapped, "you'll sweat for this!"

Canuck Bull loomed up. "What's all this? The greaser? What'd he do, jump you?"

"Just as I was crackin' down on your robbers," McLeod told him, bitterly.

Ricardo got to his feet. "What you so mad about, my fran'," he said with studied carelessness. "I have not do anything bot save your life. Don' you know that those *amigos de mío* would keel you ver' dead?"

"Friends of yours, huh?" McLeod rasped. "Fine friends they are, to go off and leave you in a jam!"

The Mexican stuck his thumbs in the broad, elaborately carved belt that he wore. "They theenk fast, those fran's of me," he said insolently. "They don' want to keel you. I geeve them their chance, they take it queeck. They are not stupid, like some others I can theenk of hombres who do not know when som'one has do them a favor, no?"

"Say!" Canuck Bull roared. "This Mex is salty, ain't he? I reckon the thing to do with him is to string him up, pronto."

The town marshal came up, weasel-faced, excited.

Canuck Bull bellowed at him. "Where you been? You always arrive up when the shootin's over. Rattle your hocks out of here.

93

We can tie hemp on this greaser without any help from the law."

"We're not hangin' this man," McLeod snapped. "Get that straight, Canuck. You, Marshal, take him in charge. He's goin' to jail an' I'm holdin' you responsible for him. Don't forget it. You may be Canuck's private lawman, but if anybody strings up this Mexican, you'll answer to me." He turned to Bull, cold-eyed. "That goes for you, too, Canuck," he warned grimly.

For an instant Bull's eyes blazed fury, then he appeared to think better of it. "It's your funeral, Slag," he said with an attempt at indifference. "If you want the greaser in jail, why jail it is."

Canuck turned and strode into the Jugtown Palace, with McLeod at his heels. The marshal, followed by a curious crowd, prodded Ricardo ahead of him with the muzzle of his six-gun.

He should have walked in the middle of street. That would have made what happened a little harder. Instead he walked along the sidewalk. A six-gun appeared out of the darkness and drove towards his head. The marshal saw it and ducked, but not in time. It landed square on his head and for him the lights went out. In the same instant six men, masked, trained six-guns on the crowd which followed. A voice snapped: "Hands up, hombres—and quick!"

Nobody resisted. The thing had been too quick and unexpected. It had taken everybody's breath away.

"Turn your backs," the same vibrant voice crackled on. "We're going down this alleyway. The first man who tries to follow is going to get hot lead for a present."

They turned. There was a scuffle of feet behind them and

when the first man found the courage to turn back, the six bandits and the Mexican were gone. Nobody attempted to follow down the alleyway. Somebody ran back down the street yelping for Marshal McLeod, but it was too late then to do anything.

CHAPTER 11
RAID ON THE HIDEOUT

RIDING THROUGH the dark, Ricky chuckled. "I don' expect you so soon," he said. "You are ver' sudden men, *no es?*"

Doc Grimson echoed his chuckle. "The boys were kind of mad at me for runnin' out on you. I had to do somethin' pretty quick."

Flint Maddox sounded shame-faced as I he said: "Hell, Doc, everybody don't think as fast as you do. I see now it was the only thing to do."

Ricky said cheerfully, "Eeef you have not go after I take all that tro'ble, I would be ver' moch disgosted."

"I'm beginnin' to like this game," Charlie Parr said. "At least we get some *dinero* out of it. Listen, I'll tell you what let's do. Tomorrow, at the crack of dawn, Slag'll be on our trail. Let's watch for him, circle him, and ride like hell to stick up that bank."

Flint groaned audibly.

"Hell," Charlie snapped in answer to the groan, "We don't have to go soft just because we've made one haul, do we?"

95

Lance grinned. "Not much danger of you goin' soft, Charlie."

"Somebody's got to be hard in this crowd," Charlie growled.

"I weel tell you a good thing," Ricardo said. "I have one nice leetle hideout, jost the other side of the Border. There ees a way to go which does not leave any track. Even thees so-good McLeod will not trail you there. Also, from a high place you can see heem coming. Then I show you a back way where you can go to Jogtown while he ees looking for you."

"I'm in favor of it, if Lon says it's all right to take the bank," Doc voted. "We got to shut Charlie up on this bank business. None of us'll have a minute's peace until we do."

Lon was silent a moment, then he said slowly: "I don't mind a bit, boys. In fact, anything that'll hurt Canuck Bull is all right with me. Only—if you don't mind, I'll stay out of this one. I—I worked there—in fact, Josh Venner don't know yet that I'm not comin' back. I'd feel like a kind of a skunk if I…."

"You'll get the name of havin' helped, anyway," Lance told him.

"Yeah, I reckon," Lon acknowledged. "But I don't care about the name. It's what I'd feel inside myself."

Lance was beginning to like this kid. In the darkness he set his jaw grimly. He was determined to find a way to clear Lon Carmody's name and send him back, self-respecting, to Jane Venner.

RICARDO LED them by devious ways to a small stream. They rode upstream about a mile until they came to a place where the water issued, apparently, from a rocky cliff.

"I am ver' sorry but here we must get our feet wet," the

Mexican apologized. They found that the brook came out of what seemed to be a small tunnel, just high enough for the passage of a horse with his head held low. Ricardo explained that the stream went underground a mile or so away and came out here. He led them into the tunnel and then unexpectedly turned right about fifteen feet from the entrance. They found themselves going up a cavernous passage at the end of which starlight showed dimly.

Charlie Parr whistled softly with admiration. "This is one of the best I ever saw," he exclaimed. "I reckon that turn to the right can't be seen from where the stream comes out."

"That ees right," Ricardo assured him, "just after we turn the top of thees tunnel it gets very low and that can be seen from outside, so nobody think it is moch use to go in there."

The passage through which they had come led directly into an arroyo which presently debouched onto high, flat land from which they descended into a grassy valley. On one side of the valley, backed up between two rocks and sheltered by brush in the front they came on a low adobe building.

At Ricardo's whistle, a dark figure got up from the doorway of the adobe and greeted them softly.

"Here, *Señores*," Ricardo told them gayly, "is your house. Be pleased to take possession of it."

"You don't mean to tell us that the creek entrance is the only way in here?" Doc asked.

"No, there ees one other," the Mexican replied. "It comes from the other way—the Mexico way. It ees not so fine, but it also ees good. Nice leetle place, no?"

He ushered them ceremoniously into the adobe, a one-room shack, nearly bare of furnishing except for a table next to a bench which ran along the wall, a bunk and one straight chair.

The Mexican who had greeted them set about preparing supper in a small shack next door, while Ricardo got out a skin of wine and a bottle of whisky.

"I theenk you wed drink the wheesky, no?" he said politely to his guests. "Me, I like better a glass of good wine."

They filled their glasses and drank to their success. By the time the Mexican cook appeared with dinner, which consisted of frijoles, tortillas and, to the American's surprise, a dozen, big, juicy steaks, they had begun to feel pretty cheerful.

"Didn't know you were runnin' a ranch here," Lance grinned.

Ricardo made a careless gesture. "Sometimes the cattle of one of our—how you say?—neighbors—comes too near by leetle valley. Then we invite heem to come in," he explained blandly. "One mus' geeve a good welcome to all of the creatures of *el Señor dios, no es?*"

When the last of the steaks had followed the final frijoles and tortillas into satisfied mouths, Doc said: "Our friend Ricardo has helped us pretty big today. I say he deserves his cut of the *dinero.*"

The others agreed heartily but Ricardo shook his head. "No! No!" he refused positively. "What I have done, I have done for fran'ship, an' also to pay a leetle debt—a so so small debt. I theenk you forget that you save my life. That ees not a ver' great thing, my leetle life. Bot to me eet ees quite valuable—I like her, my life."

He smiled engagingly, but no amount of argument could move him.

"Here," he said at last, "I weel show you." He got up and took from a shelf on the wall a small wooden box. "This, my fran's, ees what you call the opium. Eet ees not so beeg bot eet ees worth ver' moch. All my fortune ees there. Eef I have not thees leetle box, I will accept your good offer, I promise it, biccause everything I have I have pay for the stoff in thees box. Bot now, you see, I need nothing."

He put the box back on the shelf and then looked with his eyes twinkling at the faces before him. Evidently, the expressions which they were politely trying to mask told him what they were thinking.

"I know," he said. "I am not liking it moch myself. Bot what will you do? The Chinaman, he mus' have hees opium, no? Me, I don' arrange that. I am not *dios*—no! Mus' I say to the Chinaman, me, I like ver' moch my wine, my cigarillo, my *tequila*, but you, you mus' not have thees smoke you like ver' moch. Eet ees ver' bad for your health. No! I say, you are grown man—you do what you like, I do what I like. You weesh the opium, I weel sell it to you, jost like my wine-seller he sell me the good wine."

Doc Grimson grinned. "The logic," he murmured, "is flawless."

Lance looked embarrassed. "Hell, Ricky," he said, "I'm not sayin' I'd do the same thing in your place, but it's none of our business."

"Ah, *nino, nino!*" Ricardo mocked him. "Always the principles, weeth you, isn't it?"

"Well," he went on cheerfully. "Anyhow, I don' have to do

this long. This time an' maybe once more, then I go back to a leetle señorita I know. I buy myself the good ranch—I biccome ver' respectable, no? Don Ricardo, the beeg *ranchero*—yes?"

IT HAPPENED about ten minutes later. Doc had said: "Well, since Ricardo is too wealthy to need any *dinero*, we'll divide it up among ourselves. Charlie, you and Flint come and help me count."

The three were seated at the table, therefore, with the money spread before them. Lance and Ricardo were talking in low tones on the bunk. Lon Carmody occupied the straight chair, staring moodily at the floor. Lockjaw, replete with whisky, wine and beefsteak was on the floor in a corner, his back against the wall, already beginning to snore a little.

A voice rasped from the doorway. "You're covered from both windows. Put 'em up!" Slag McLeod stood there, a six-gun in each hand and a look on his face that told them the first man to make a false move was going to die. Behind him, at either side, was a man with a Winchester, and the barrels of these rifles were also trained on the group inside.

Doc Grimson put up his hands. "Hello, Slag," he said pleasantly. "We didn't expect you until morning."

The others put up their hands, too. McLeod walked into the room and said "Come in, boys. They're gonna behave."

Lockjaw chose that moment to wake up. His eyes came open blearily. He stared, grabbed the gun at his side and started to scramble to his feet. "Hold it, Lockjaw!" Charlie Parr warned sharply.

Lockjaw put the gun back on the floor and fell back into the corner. It was just in time, because the finger of one of the men outside had begun to tighten on the trigger of his Winchester.

Slag McLeod laughed with dry satisfaction. "I thought you'd come here," he said. "I've had Ricardo's little hideout marked down for some time, meanin' to pull him in the next time he tried anything. I'd have taken him a long time ago, except that I knew he wasn't the big feller and I hoped the trail would lead to him. It's been only recently that I figgured it out that Ricardo was operatin' on his own."

Doc Grimson leaned back carelessly against the wall. "Well," he said calmly, "you were smarter than we figured, McLeod. You've got us, an' got us with the goods." He motioned with his head toward the money in front of him. "There's the *dinero,* and here—" one of his raised hands reached up to the shelf behind him. Instantly, every gun in the room—and there were a good many of them, since the other four had come in—jumped nervously toward him. Doc grinned. "Don't get nervous, boys," he said, reassuringly. "I'm not trying any funny play. I'm just getting the opium."

His hand caught hold of the box and tossed it on the table before him. "You'd find it anyway," he drawled, "so I'm savin' you the trouble."

Slag McLeod looked at him with narrowed eyes. "You swear that's opium, Doc?" It was evident that he was suspicious of the box.

Doc laughed. "It won't bite you, Slag," he said, amused. "But if you want my word on it, why you can have it—that's opium."

McLeod said grimly, "I dunno why you're givin' it to me, but

I do know that the one thing about you is your word." He holstered his left gun and came up to the table, the right gun trained directly on Doc. His eyes, too, remained fixed on the man in front of him, while his left hand groped for the package.

Doc laughed. "Somebody's made you mistake-shy, Slag," he said mockingly. "Be careful there's not a sidewinder in that box."

Slag McLeod straightened up, the faintest expression of annoyance on his granite features. That word "mistake-shy" had evidently gotten under his skin. Then, for the fraction of a second his eyes flicked to the box he held in hand. It was the moment that Doc Grimson had waited for. His foot, held against the center piece under the table, shot out. At the same instant, he flung himself sideways. McLeod's gun roared, but the edge of the table, driven against his thighs, shook his hand. The shot thudded into the wall over Doc's head.

Like driven pistons, Doc's hands had come down as he moved. Almost before the marshal's gun went off, Doc gripped the edge of the table. Now he sent it hurtling more heavily against Slag's legs, over-turning it in the same moment. The lamp crashed to the floor, went out.

DOC'S LIGHTNING movement had been unexpected enough to take everybody by surprise and the staggering form of the marshal in front of them had embarrassed his men just that fatal fraction of a second which enabled the Mavericks to get in motion. Flint and Charlie Parr flung themselves sideways, ducking, as the guns began to talk. But Doc jumped squarely for McLeod, shielding himself, at the same time, reaching for his guns. The Colts came out as the lamp struck the floor, and just as the room went dark, one of them crashed on the marshal's skull.

Then the room was filled with the suffocating fumes of burnt powder and vicious stabs of orange flame as Colts and Winchesters beat a deafening thunder. A dozen men burning powder in a room fifteen by ten. It was pandemonium.

But it lasted only a few short seconds. There was the grunt and heavy fall of a badly hit man; the sharp, agonized exclamation of another, then a flying body was outlined briefly against the doorway and disappeared in the dark outside. It was followed in quick succession by another and another, until five in all had gone out. The fifth stopped outside to fire several times then, for a long moment, there was silence, broken only by the shuddering breath of the man who had been badly hit and the groans, louder but less disquieting of the other. Then Doc's voice said, "I think that's all." As he spoke there was the sound of racing hoofs dying off in the distance. He struck a match, holding it high over his head.

"Anybody hurt?"

"Don't think so," Charlie Parr told him. "Got another lamp, Ricardo?"

Lance called from outside: "They've gone, fannin' the breeze plain and fancy."

He had been the fifth man through the door.

They found candles on the shelf and took stock of the damages. Flint had been creased in the arm and Ricardo had taken a slight leg wound. None of the others was even scratched.

Doc Grimson turned his attention to the wounded members

of the other crowd. Slag McLeod was still unconscious, though, apparently, not seriously hurt. One of the others was shot through the chest and his partner had a shattered hip.

"Better tie McLeod up," Doc suggested. "It'll make things easier for us all around if he's not loose to interfere during the next couple of days."

Charlie Parr set about the task, while Flint helped Doc take care of the other two. The latter shook his head over the man who was shot through the chest. "With luck, he'll pull through," he said, "but it'll take some luck." The other's wound, though painful, would not be dangerous unless infection set in.

"What about staying here?" Lance asked, when Doc had finished his dressings. "They're liable to be back with help pretty quick, aren't they."

Ricardo shrugged. "I don't theenk tonight," he said. "They weel know we are looking for it. Bot that is nothing. They don't know the water entrance, I theenk. They came from the Mexico side. To do that they mus' pass through a canyon that one man can hold against an army. We put a guard there, then we can sleep in peace."

The table still lay on its side. Ricardo set it up, then stared. *"Caramba!"* he swore suddenly. "The opium—where is it?"

CHAPTER 12
SMUGGLERS SYNDICATE

THE WOODEN box was nowhere to be found. Charlie Parr recalled vaguely having noticed a noise down behind the table where McLeod lay, but nobody had fired from there so he had paid no attention to it. The only possible conclusion was that one of the four men who had escaped had snatched up the box containing the opium before he had leaped through the doorway.

Ricardo swore briefly and savagely in Spanish. "All those men with McLeod were Canuck Bull's men," he said. "I do not think they have taken that opium for evidence." He gritted his teeth, his eyes blazing with helpless fury.

Then he controlled himself, recovered his pose of nonchalance. "Well," he said, nipping his hand in the air, "there eet goes—all of it. Nothing to do, I theenk, an' when there ees nothing to do, one mus' do—nothing. I theenk I go now an' see what they have done to Pedro. He was in the cook shack, washing the plates. I theenk he will not stay out of thees fight unless they have gotten him."

He sauntered out, carelessly, but the others saw that when he had passed the doorway there was a sudden sag to his shoulders.

"Wiped out," Lance said softly. "No more little señorita, and no more big rancho."

"And our fault," Flint put in.

The Five looked at one another. Then, as though by a kind of telepathy, their eyes went to the money, which was still scattered on the floor. Nobody said anything for a moment, then one by one the others glanced at Charlie Parr and hastily looked away. Charlie raised resigned eyes to heaven.

"All right! All right! All right!" he said, glaring at them. "Give

Canuck Bull's colt leveled....

Thundered, spitting flame at Lon.

it to him. Give it all to him. I didn't say anything against it, did I? But listen to me and listen to me plenty—tomorrow we're gonna take that bank!"

Doc Grimson grinned faintly and got down and began gathering up the money. There was a lot of it. When he got it together he handed it in silence to Charlie, who took it, growling.

"All right with, you, Lon?" Doc asked.

Lon Carmody looked at them wondering. He was still shaken

and excited by the fight. But what occupied him most was the fact that he had not been scared. Doc's sudden movement had caught him as much off guard as it had the posse-men. He had not moved at all until the lamp hit the floor, then automatically he had gone for his gun and begun to fan shots at the flashes that came from where the posse had been standing. He hadn't been scared at all—just occupied with shooting. He had pretended afterwards to be taking an interest in the proceedings but he hadn't really. He was too full of excited wonder at himself. From time to time, surreptitiously, he reached down to feel the warmth that came through the holster from the hot barrel of his gun.

Now, when he found himself addressed, he said, "Sure! Sure!" It was something about giving Ricky his share of the money. Lon didn't care about the money....

Ricardo came back. "They knocked him on the head," he said, with an attempt at cheerfulness. "He weel be all right. He has a hard head, this Pedro."

Charlie Parr held out the money to him. "Here! This is yours," he said gruffly.

Ricardo stared at the money. "But, amigo…" he began to protest. Charlie took his hand roughly and pressed the money into it. "Take it," he snapped. "We've brought you some hard luck and we're sharin' with you."

"But—but," Ricardo said, holding the money helplessly, "this is all of it. You…."

"We got our share," Charlie told him curtly. "That's for you an' the little señorita. Don't lemme hear any more out of you!"

Lon understood then. His head came up and his chest lifted. After all, he had fought shoulder-to-shoulder with these men. He, too, was a part of the gang which was capable of a careless gesture like this.

Ricardo looked at them with his black eyes suddenly gone soft.

"I had one fran'," he said softly. "Now I think I have seex. That is too moch good fortune for one man."

Lance Clayton stepped quietly out of the doorway. An idea had just come to him. The man who had taken the opium was one of Canuck Bull's men. Would he be taking his find to the mine? Why not go up and see? There, was more chance now at night than there would be in the day-time.

He slipped out to Ricardo's small corral and whistled softly to the stallion. When the big horse came nosing up to him, Lance threw Ricky's spare saddle on him and took him quietly up the slope to the arroyo which led to the creek tunnel. No use getting the others in on this. It was his own job. He had gotten them into enough trouble as it was—and he had no way of knowing how this *pasear* would work out. If he could prove that Canuck Bull's men were the smugglers he might be able to use it to get Lon Carmody out of the hole the Mavericks had dragged him into. It was a slim chance—but the only chance of saving Lon from outlawry. Lance had to take it—alone.

CANUCK BULL'S silver mine, Lance knew, lay some distance out of Jugtown and fairly near the Border. That latter fact had been Bull's excuse for keeping it so heavily guarded. Thinking it over, Lance was surprised that no one had suspected the big Canadian before. But then, as Jane Venner had said, it was not considered healthy in Jugtown to do too much speculating about Bull's activities. He had the town marshal in his pocket—and it was said that the sheriff had shown himself friendly to the boss of Jugtown on more than one occasion. The fact that the big man apparently employed an army of nearly two score gunmen might be suspicious, but it was not proof of anything. And no one, unless it was Slag McLeod, was likely to inquire too closely into the army's activities and duties. It was enough that Canuck Bull was plenty dangerous and that his gunmen made him practically invincible.

Riding through the night towards the mine, Lance reflected grimly that Bull's army had recently been somewhat cut down. That fight on the mesa and this last fracas in Ricky's hideout had reduced Bull's effective force considerably. If Lance's guess was good, it would be still further reduced before the Mavericks were done with Bull.

He had, he knew, about two hours' fast ride from the hideout to the mine, so he kept the stallion at a brisk pace, cutting cross-country. As always, when he had to go somewhere in a hurry on the big horse, his heart swelled with pleasure and pride in the long, tireless stride with which Tomahawk ate up the miles, and the sure-footedness with which he traveled over rough country. The stallion apparently had the eyes of a cat. He faltered and hesitated no more at night than he did in broad daylight—which was not at all.

The night was moonless. Only the dim radiance of the big southwestern stars picked out the main features of the landscape and brought into shadowy relief rocks and clumps of brush which might spell danger. Lance rode with eyes and ears strained. Night-riding in a smuggling country was never altogether safe. In Lance's situation it might turn out to be very dangerous, indeed.

But he had encountered no one when, at the end of two

hours, he came in sight of the long hog-back on whose slopes the mine lay. Here, he pulled the stallion to a walk and proceeded cautiously. He had never seen the mine and had only Ricky's description to go on. Presently he came to the edge of a twisting arroyo which the Mexican had told him about and rode Tomahawk down into it. Once in the shadow of the bottom he dismounted and ground-tied the stallion. For a few seconds he whispered softly in the horse's ear, giving his voice an urgent and secret quality. Then he turned and climbed up the back, satisfied that Tomahawk would not move or whinny.

The mine itself was still more than a quarter of a mile away, according to Ricky's description, but Lance moved forward with the same careful stealth as another man might have used in the final hundred yards. Everything depended, he knew, on being able to locate the guards without being seen, and somehow to find a way past them. Beyond that, he had no plan.

He had traversed about two hundred yards when suddenly he stepped softly into the center of a clump of bushes and waited in silence. He had caught a muffled beat of hoofs somewhere in the distance. The riders, whoever they were, were coming his way, and as the seconds passed it became apparent that they were coming along a course which might bring them directly by him. He stepped a little further into the clump of brush and squatted down.

As he did so, something stirred suddenly under his foot and slapped against the side of his boot. His pulses jumped and the sweat came out on his forehead. The thing near him might be a rattler or a gila monster. But he dared not stir. The horsemen were very close now. Then he saw it—a sluggish, squat, lizard-like shape, not two feet away from him. Impossible to tell in that light whether it was a Gila or a chuckwalla. It was sitting there looking at him, motionless.

LANCE BEGAN to understand the way Canuck Bull might feel, and grinned at himself for it. Then four riders pounded up and the lizard moved away. Lance breathed easier.

He could not see in the darkness who the riders were, but there was something vaguely familiar about their figures, and the fact that there were four of them set Lance's heart pounding. Four men had escaped from the fight in the hideout....

Suddenly one of the riders spoke: "The boys are goin' to open their eyes at this haul," he said.

One of the others laughed. "Especially, when they hear how you grabbed it off, Jake—with McLeod there an' all."

"The big boy's got to come through handsome for it, too," a third spoke up.

The first man spoke again as they rode past, his words unintelligible now, but Lance had heard enough. His hunch had been correct—they were bringing the opium to the mine. That made it certain that this was smuggling headquarters. He went on faster now, following in the traces of the riders.

"That's far enough," a voice cracked out some distance ahead: "Who is it?"

The riders pulled up. "It's Jake and three of the boys," one of them answered.

"You sound like Jake," the guard answered, "but I better have a look at you. Come up along." It was evident that he meant to take no chances.

Lance kept moving, slipping from cover to cover, silently, but covering ground rapidly. He wanted to get as close behind the group as possible while they moved in. That would enable him to spot the guard and see the way the others took to get to the mine buildings.

He was taking a chance of being spotted, of course, but he was counting on the others' attention being fixed on Jake and the guard. He came up to within a dozen yards of the mounted group.

In a moment, the man called Jake called: "Come on, boys," and the three rode in to join him and the guard. Lance could make out the figure of the guard now, and when the four men had ridden in he saw the man take a seat on what appeared to be a rock. In a moment, the brief flare of a match half-revealed his features under the big sombrero. Then the glowing end of a lighted cigarette showed his location.

The man, Jake, called out something which Lance did not catch, and a sleepy voice replied to him. In a moment, a light appeared which threw into dim relief several adobe shacks and the figures of the four men who had dismounted. An interval of excited talk followed and then all the men disappeared into one of the buildings. The door closed behind them and the only light remaining came from a small window in the side of the building.

Lance waited, but there was no sign of any other guard. If there was one, he must be on the other side of the camp. He considered trying to sneak up on the man before him but almost at once realized the hopelessness of it. In the dead stillness of the night, the slightest movement would be heard. He could never hope to knock the guard on the head before he took alarm and aroused the others.

There was only one thing to do; he must take a chance on being able to slip between this guard and whatever one might be on watch at the side of the camp.

So he began to crawl cautiously backward. When he thought he had put a safe distance between himself and the guard he circled and came in again, quartering. This manoeuver enabled him to approach the buildings from an angle toward which the guard's back was turned.

Pulses pounding, he crept in. When he had gotten directly behind the seated man's back and as close to the buildings as he was, the guard got up and began to walk. His beat led away from Lance for the first few steps, then turned toward him. The Maverick shrank into the shelter of a mesquite bush and sat immobile. The guard came up, still smoking his cigarette until he was within a few feet of the bush behind which Lance crouched. Lance tensed, ready to spring, knowing that if the other came a step farther he would be discovered, and knowing too that he must hit hard and suddenly to prevent an outcry.

The guard stopped, seemed to be looking directly at the bush, then calmly turned his back and walked in the other direction. Lance stole forward softly, intensely conscious of the whisper of his feet on the soft top-soil, and expecting every moment that the other would hear him. But the guard apparently noticed nothing. He walked to the end of his beat and turned.

Lance lay flat on the ground, scarcely breathing. When the guard turned again, he stole on. He had gotten, by these tactics, almost to the lighted building when a beat of hoofs sent him to cover again.

Evidently, there were a considerable number of riders approaching the place. They rode in at a trot, were halted by the guard and then permitted to go on.

AS THEY passed between the buildings Lance could make out perhaps a dozen figures. The door of the adobe swung open and a man came out with a lantern. "Hullo, Bill," he said, "you got 'em, did you?"

The lantern showed that eight of the mounted figures were Chinese. The man addressed as Bill got down from his horse. "Yeah," he said. "Had to tie about half the yellow devils on their broncs. They kept fallin' off."

The four who had ridden in with the opium came out, and Jake said: "We got somethin' they'll like tonight."

"Only they don't get it," the man with the lantern said. "Throw 'em into the small shack. They go out with the rest of the goods in the mornin'."

The other man said to the Chinamen. "You go in there. Stay all time. No come out at all—hear?"

"The first time I see one of your noses, you heathen devils, I'm gonna shoot it off. Git, now!"

Bill said: "They run in two extra ones on us. You got enough coffins?"

115

"Yeah," the man with the lantern said, nodding toward a nearby pile of wooden boxes. Lance saw that there were nearly a dozen of them—boxes roughly built of pine and coffin-like in shape. One of them was in a position where he could see a row of holes drilled in the bottom.

"See you're puttin' holes in 'em now," Bill remarked.

"Yeah," the other told him carelessly. "We got holes drilled in the bottom of the wagons, too. That way they'll get some air. One of 'em died last trip. They was clear up to Leadville with 'em an' was unloadin' there at Crazy Mike's place. They had to turn around and go clear out of town so they could plant the devil. Things like that loses us time an' money."

Lance pursed his lips in a soundless whistle. He understood now that they put Chinamen in the "coffins," into ore wagons, covered them with ore and thus were able to transport them a long way inland before turning them loose. It was a clever plan, for it distracted suspicion from Canuck Bull and Jugtown. Wandering Chinaman who might be suspected of being "wet" were not found around the home locality and could not be traced back to it.

Jake said: "Well, we got to ride. Canuck's got to be told what happened tonight."

The four who had brought the opium mounted and rode off, while the men who had brought the Chinamen unsaddled and went into the adobe.

Lance had learned all he needed to know. No doubt the wisest thing to do would be to get back and tell the others. If he could somehow get Slag McLeod to ride against the mine, the Five Mavericks would lend their aid. It was, however, not far from dawn. They would have to come in daylight and they would have to fight. Including the guard, there were at least six men here. Forted up, they could hold the mine a long time—long enough, perhaps, for word to get back to Canuck Bull and the rest of his men.

Then, too, before he was able to get back with the others, the wagons might be on their way. Of course, they could be trailed but Lance had heard that they traveled always under heavy guard, so the problem of taking them would be a good deal like that of capturing the mine. Moreover, it was against Lance's instincts to run for help. The idea came to him that he might be able to handle the whole thing himself.

Lance could smell the odor of coffee coming from the shack. He figured that the men were probably eating, and that if he could find some way to get rid of the guard, he might be able to walk into the door of the cabin, throw his Colts on the men there and take the whole gang at once.

The guard was the real problem. Lance could hear him and vaguely see him as he walked his post. He had the air of a man who was entirely wide awake.

Then Lance found the answer. He was between the guard and the cabin. He had only to steal in among the buildings and then come strolling out. The guard wouldn't suspect him until he got so close that suspecting him wouldn't do any good. The only real danger was that the men in the cabin might hear his footsteps and come to investigate. That was a chance that had to be taken. Probably, they would be too busy talking and eating to pay any attention to the slight sounds that he would make. HE WAITED until the guard's beat took him in the other direction and slipped in toward the cabin. He could heard the men inside laughing and talking. He started to walk quietly out toward the guard, strolling casually but trying to make as little noise as possible. The guard saw him when he was about halfway there and stopped. He stared toward Lance a moment without speaking, and there was something in his attitude which told that he was suspicious. He realized suddenly that the cabin door had not opened and that the guard would have been sure to notice it if it had.

"Who's that?" The man's voice confirmed Lance's impression. He was suspicious, all right.

Lance's pulses began to pound and the nerves of his arm crisped and tingled as they always did before the draw. It looked as though it were going to be necessary to shoot it out with this fellow and then run for it. The others would come piling out at the first hint of trouble.

He laughed and said: "You gettin' nervous? Keep your eye out front and you'll be all right."

As he talked he kept coming.

The man had brought his rifle up to the ready and Lance could see that he was peering at him doubtfully.

"That you Curly?" he asked. Lance could see he couldn't believe that it was Curly. He said: "You gone loco? Since when did I begin to look like Curly?"

Automatically, the guard lowered the point of his rifle, dropping it into the hollow of his arm, lulled into a sense of security by the joking casualness of Lance's manner.

"Danged if I mustn't be—" he began, and then stopped, finding himself looking into the barrels of a couple of business-like Colts.

"Don't make a sound," Lance told him in a low voice, "unless you want a one-way ticket to hell."

Even in the darkness Lance could see the way the man's jaw dropped open.

He took the rifle and then made the fellow turn around while he relieved him of his six-guns. Then he hesitated. He knew he ought to knock the man out, but it went against his grain to hit an unarmed man. Still, the odds against him were too great. He holstered his right gun and his fist whipped up to land just under the guard's ear. The man grunted and his knees buckled. Lance caught him as he fell.

Swiftly, he slipped back to the buildings, got a rope and bound and gagged his prisoner. Then he eased toward the door of the cabin. He knew that he was taking a big chance. There must be a guard or so stationed on the other side of the mine, though he had seen no sign of them. But he thought he could take the men in the cabin without any noise. That done, he could go out looking for the other guard. One man wouldn't be enough to bother him.

At the door of the cabin he paused, listening. From the sounds he concluded that the men there had finished their meal and were about to go to bed. He flung the door wide and stepped in fast, a six-gun in either hand. "Get 'em high," he snapped. "Your game's up."

He had a momentary vision of the room, of four startled faces staring at him, of a couple of pairs of hands starting to lift, then the door he had flung open swung back on him, hard-driven, knocking him nearly off his feet. He realized as it happened that the fifth man must have been standing or sitting behind the door and had had the quickness of mind to kick it rebounding against the opener.

From then on things happened fast. Lance bounced from the door-jamb, slipping sideways just in time to avoid a bullet which came crashing through the door. Just as he leveled his guns again, a skillet, thrown with fierce accuracy, caught him in the face, stunning him. The nearest man to him jumped for him, knocking his right gun from his hand with a downward slash of the open palm which paralyzed his forearm. Without pause, the same adversary seized his left gun in a two-handed grip.

But by that time Lance had recovered a little from the effect of the blow from the skillet. He was aware that the others were rushing him, as he brought a knee up to the stomach of the man who held his gun. The man grunted and looked sick but he hung to the gun like a bulldog. A fist flashed over his shoulder and landed with sledgehammer force on Lance's jaw. As he staggered back, his grip on the gun loosened a little and it came loose on the other man's hand, exploding as it did so. The recoil of the gun kicked it from the grip of the man who held it and it fell to the floor.

Lance came back hard. He drove his right to the eye of the man who had hit him and sent a hard left to the stomach of another. From then on the room was a wild confusion of straggling bodies and flying fists. The men in that place were gunmen, but they had laid their guns aside for ease, and now things were at too close quarters for guns. They had to use their hands, and keep using them fast, against this big-shouldered, lithe-hipped young man who twisted like a wild-cat and charged like an infuriated steer.

The pace was too furious for accurate hitting. Half a dozen times, Lance's right ripped over like exploding dynamite, to send someone hurtling back against the wall, but each time the man came back, dazed but not knocked out.

A heavy-shouldered, ape-armed man rushed hard from the side, took a left that sent him caroming off with a split cheek, but swung back and jumped Lance from behind. The latter twisted, gave, and sent the man sailing over his shoulders. His fall knocked down two of the others. Like a flash, Lance leapt toward a fourth, sending his right flashing through to the point of the jaw. The man's knees buckled and he went down, to stay down. But in the same instant the remaining man had dived for Lance's knees, nearly knocking him from his feet. Ineffectually the Maverick struggled to free himself, slashing lefts for the other's head, but the man clung like a leech, and two of the others were on their feet now, coming in. A savage left stopped one in his tracks, but the other drove on, clinching. Then the ape-armed man, scrambling for Lance's fallen gun, got it and brought it crashing down on the Maverick's head. The room exploded around him in a great blaze of light and he went down into darkness….

CHAPTER 13
GUN-HOSTAGE!

W HEN HE regained consciousness, he was lying on the floor, bound hand and foot, and with a head which ached as though all the hammers of hell were beating in it. The five men in the room had been joined by a sixth, whom Lance had never seen before and who, he guessed, was the guard who had been on duty at the other side of the camp.

The ape-armed man was saying: "You better get on back to your post, Joe. I don't know where the rest of these fellers are, but they ain't never very far apart. The other four are apt to breeze in here sudden, and if they do they'll come a-shootin'. Keep a sharp eye out."

The guard said: "All right," and went out. He didn't look very enthusiastic about it.

Ape-arm called after him: "I'm goin' to send some more of the boys out after you. You'll each take a side of the camp and walk along it until you meet each other. That way you'll all be in touch in case they try to get through."

Lance saw that the guard he had knocked out was also in the room. Ape-arm said to him: "Git on back to your place an' don't make no more mistakes. Mick, you take the east side, and Fred, you take the west. Walk close in, so none of the four of you will be far apart any of the time. The rest of us'll be here with the door open, so as to come swarmin' out the first thing that happens."

The men designated got their rifles, buckled on their guns and went out.

Ape-arm's glance fell on Lance and he saw that the prisoner's eyes were open. "So you waked up, did you?" he snarled. "Well, it ain't for long. Where are those partners of yours?"

"I bet you wish you knew," Lance told him with a sardonic grin.

Deliberately the man kicked him in the stomach. Lance gasped and doubled up. "Pretty salty, ain't you," his captor growled. "We'll soon take that out of you. Where are your partners?"

Lance gasped painfully, "You'll find out—just before—they cut your heart out."

Ape-arm kicked him in the face. "Don't talk, then," he snarled. "There'll be somebody here in an hour that'll tell whether you're goin' to be given a chance to talk before you die or whether you're gonna die first. Either way, it don't make no difference."

LANCE GROUND his teeth and was silent. He knew that it would be dawn in an hour. Evidently they intended to send for Canuck Bull as soon as daylight made it safe. And Lance knew he could expect little mercy, once the boss of Jugtown realized that he knew the secret of the mine. His own crowd would probably not even begin to be restless about him until he didn't show up in time for the bank robbery. They might find their way to the mine then, but it would be too late.

He felt like groaning aloud. He had bungled everything. It

was not so much that he was about to lose his own life, he had, in addition, failed in all the plans about Lon Carmody and Jane. Carmody would continue to be a hunted man. Jane Venner would be at the mercy of Canuck Bull. The remainder of the Mavericks would have Slag McLeod on their trail until the latter died or the four went to jail. And all because he, Lance, had conceived a hair-brained scheme and then messed things up dismally. He deserved to die. He deserved anything that came to him.

But Lance was not dead yet, and even as he thought all this, a part of his mind was busy with possible ways out. Automatically, he strained at his bonds. It was then that he realized for the first time that he was bound with wire. It had been wound around his legs at the knees and ankles and about his arms at the elbows and wrists. Not much chance of working loose from that!

A short, swarthy man with a broken nose said, scowling, "What's the use of waiting for the big feller? This jasper knows enough to send us all up for a long stretch. I'm for ventilatin' him, pronto."

"Shore!" agreed the third man. "We can allus say we had to shoot him to keep him from gittin' away. What's Canuck want to see him for anyhow?"

Ape-arm thoughtfully scratched his bristly chin. "Well, I dunno," he said doubtfully. "The boss says he don't want no killin' that ain't needful. It'd maybe be better to let him decide on this one himself."

"Hell, he can't let the jigger go. It's too dangerous. We better git rid of him before anythin' happens to make it harder. I don't feel easy with the rest of that gang around and us not knowin' where they are. Kill him now, and we won't have no regrets."

"Shore!" the swarthy man assented eagerly. "Dead men don't do no talkin'. Let's git it over with."

The ape-arm man appeared shaken. "We could bury him down in the mine," he said thoughtfully. "Wouldn't nobody ever find him down in the old shaft. Well—maybe you're right. How'll we do it?"

There was some hesitation over this, then the swarthy one said: "Let's shoot him in the back, then we can tell Bull he got loose and tried to run for it. After he's dead we can take the wire off him and bury him down in the old shaft."

The third man said: "Maybe we better hang him. I—dang me, if I didn't always hate to shoot a hombre in the back."

The swarthy man sneered. "You're gittin' soft, ain't you? Don't worry, I'll do the shootin'."

He slid a Colt from its holster and walked around behind Lance. The other two moved aside, so as to be out of the line of fire—just in case.

The ape-armed man said: "You got anythin' to say before you go?"

Lance's brain raced. "Yeah," he said. "I've got plenty to say."

"Make it short, then. We ain't got much time to waste."

"You wanted to know where my partners were, didn't you. Well, I'll tell you somethin' you don't know. We've got Canuck Bull where we want him. I'm not the only one that's got a line on this mine an' what goes on in it. When daylight comes, my partners'll be here—they may be here any minute. They'll be bringin' Slag McLeod. This whole game is up, here. If you kill me, they'll look until they find my body. An' there won't any of 'em rest until they send the whole gang of you to hell after me. You better get onto yourself in time. Canuck Bull is…."

The swarthy man snarled. "Talk! I'm gonna shut him up now."

Lance heard the hammer of the six-gun click as it went back.

The ape-armed man looked doubtful. "Well, I dunno," he said.

The swarthy one exclaimed impatiently. "What in blazes is the matter with you? These Mavericks have got you bluffed, haven't they? What if they do come? They'll get a dose of hot lead, that's all. An' this skunk's goin' to get his, right now!"

Lance drew his breath and opened his mouth to start talking again. Not that there was much use in it, but if only he could gain a few minutes, maybe….

He could hear the man had knelt behind him leveling the Colt.

A voice spoke from the doorway. "Uncock that gun, and do it quick an' careful!" The words were spoken in a low tone with a curious, compelling vibrancy in it. If they had been shouted the effect could not have been so overwhelmingly deadly.

Lance let out his breath in a quick gasp of relief. He was aware that the sweat had come out on his forehead and that the room had gone excessively still, as though the men in it had been chilled into immobility and silence by that sudden voice.

From where he lay he could see the doorway and Doc

Grimson standing there, with Charlie Parr beside him. The lamplight glittered on the barrels of Doc's six-guns where the bluing had worn off from constant use.

"Uncock it and put it on the floor—quick!" Doc warned, still in that soft, deadly voice. "If you hesitate another instant, I'll blow you to hell, you murdering skunk."

Behind Lance the hammer of the six-gun went down with a little click and he heard the gun itself laid on the floor.

"Get your hands up, all of you!" Doc snapped then.

The hands went up.

A sudden shot broke the silence of the night outside, followed by another, the two so close together that they sounded almost like one. After that there was silence.

Charlie Parr came over and began to take the wire off Lance. By way of replying to the question in his eyes, he said: "I reckon one of the guards got ambitious. We come up just as they were comin' out and threw down on two of 'em that walked out together. The other boys went off to sneak up on the other two while Doc and me come here."

Doc Grimson, who had been busy disarming the men in the room, said, "Looks like we got here just about in time. You ought to leave word when you're going to tackle a whole mining camp by yourself."

Lance looked sheepish. "I wanted to keep you out of it," he said, and explained what had happened to him. "How'd you happen to come on?" he asked, when he had finished.

Doc grinned. "Oh, Charlie got all het up for fear you'd be too late for the bank robbery tomorrow, and Ricky told us you had got kind of interested in the mine, so we thought we better amble out and see how you came out."

THE OTHERS came in, Ricky among them, and with them, three of the guards. Lockjaw explained under questioning that the other guard had had an accident. "He shot first," he said, "but I reckon he was nervous, or somethin'."

Charlie Parr asked irritably: "Now what? We've got these buzzards—what are we gonna do with 'em?"

Lance, stamping up and down to restore the circulation to his legs, told him about the Chinamen in the other shack and the "coffins."

"We've got the deadwood on Canuck Bull," he ended. "What I say is do this: Let's send Lon with a note to Slag, telling him to come here. Lon can tell him what he'll find when he gets here and then let him loose. We'll wait here, with these hombres tied up and the Chinks locked in, until Slag heaves in sight, then we'll fan the breeze, goin' out the back way. My guess is that Slag's goin' to think we've been plenty of help in this business. He may even decide that he can't see our tracks as good as he used to. I dunno. But Lon, you tell him that it was you that got wind of Bull's bein' a *contrabandista*, that you asked us to help you run it down an' that we had to try to get away from that posse of Bull's men up on the mesa in order to go on with what we were doin'. Tell him we knew we were fighting a gang of smugglers, even though they were his deputies. Tell him that if it hadn't been for that, you, bein' a law-abidin' citizen, wouldn't have resisted arrest. I'm bettin' he'll be willin' to forget the whole business."

"I believe you're right, Lance," Doc agreed instantly. "Slag'll forget Lon's part in it. It'll be a big feather in Marshal McLeod's hat to bust up this gang. He's goin' to be willing to forget a lot."

"Fine!" grunted Charlie Parr, with a hint of irony, "maybe he'll even forget it was us when he finds out that somebody robbed the bank today."

"What about Canuck Bull?" Flint asked, eyeing Lance. "You leavin' it to Slag to arrest him."

"No," Lance told him, setting his jaw, "I'm not."

He knew what Flint meant. Flint was wondering if he had changed his mind about trying to give Lon Carmody nerve enough to go up against the man who had whipped and disgraced him.

He put a friendly hand on Lon Carmody's shoulder and led him outside. When they were alone, he said grimly, "Lon, the time's come. You've got to get Canuck now—or never. If you wait, Slag McLeod'll have him dead or behind the bars, and you'll never get your chance. How about it—are you willin' to go up against him? Or are you goin' to know for the rest of your life that you didn't have the guts to?"

Lon Carmody looked at him queerly in the dim light which came from the doorway. "You—you knew all that all along?" he asked.

"We all knew it," Lance told him. "We took you with us because we thought maybe you had good enough stuff in you to get over bein' gunshy, if you got the chance."

"An'—you took me in just the same?" Lon asked wonderingly.

129

"Listen," Lance told him. "Any man can get the nerve knocked out of him once. If he can make a comeback from it, it shows he's got more natural nerve than average. We thought we'd see. You're plenty fast enough to go up against Canuck. If you do it and get him, you'll be a man again. If you don't you'll always be the way you were. Your life won't be worth anything to you or to anybody else. What's it to be?"

Lon Carmody drew a long breath. "I'll tell you what it's to be. I'll go up against Canuck. I'll go up against him today, as fast as I can ride to town. I'll get him or he'll get me."

Lance put out his hand. "I guess we wasn't wrong," he said softly. "Put it there, Lon."

Later Lon Carmody was to ask himself just why the Five Mavericks should have taken so much interest in him and his problem, but just at that moment, he was too taken up with his sudden determination to think of anything else.

"You get on your bronc and go let Slag McLeod loose," Lance told him. "Then you ride to town. Go in and hide up. Get a friend of yours to spread the word that you're comin' into town at noon sharp to kill Canuck Bull. Write a note to Canuck yourself. Tell him you've been waiting three years to kill him and that today's the day. Tell him you're goin' to be in front of the Palace at twelve o'clock. We'll be there, to see fair play. All right?"

Lon Carmody set his jaw and straightened his shoulders. "All right," he said. "I'll do it that way."

"Fork your bronc, then, amigo. We'll see you at twelve o'clock."

THE OTHER turned away to go toward the ravine where

they had left their horses. Then Charlie Parr called after him. "Wait a minute, Lon."

"Listen," he said gravely, when he was close to Carmody again. "You oughta be fast enough to kill Canuck, but nobody can be sure of that. Do you realize what you're doin'? Maybe it'll be you that gets lead-poisonin' instead."

Lon said grimly. "I realize it."

"An' you're willin' to risk it?" Charlie asked.

"I shore am."

Charlie put both hands on Lon's shoulders and gripped hard. "You'll get him, boy. Keep your nerve—we're backin' you strong."

Lon's voice was suddenly husky as he said: "I'm not tryin' to thank you—or the others. But I won't be losin' my nerve, an' I want you to know, if anything—happens, that it was worth it—plenty worth it!"

When Lon had left, Doc Grimson looked grave.

"I wonder if we've been right about this," he said. "It looks like we'll be murderin' that kid. I—he's a kind of a nice kid—I hate to see it."

Lance set his jaw and his eyes were hard. "Jane Venner's got a right to a real man," he said grimly. "She gets one—or nothin'."

Charlie Parr said: "A gunsmoke cure is the only cure. But how do you know she wouldn't rather have him alive an' yeller than dead and brave? You can't count on a woman."

"I never did see what it was all about," Lockjaw put in. "Why don't you just take her yourself, Lance, an' let this jasper go to hell?"

"That'd be easier," Lance muttered, his eyes suddenly bitter. "This way, I lose—no matter what way it comes out."

"Huh?" Lockjaw asked, staring. "I don't see that. If this jasper gets ventilated...."

Flint kicked him and he broke off. Lance turned away.

"What'd I say now?" Lockjaw asked indignantly when Lance was out of earshot.

But Flint didn't answer. He didn't think there was much chance of explaining to Lockjaw that Lance had had to give the girl up in his own mind before he could let Carmody risk being killed. Fine points of honor like that were not able to pierce the tough hide of Lockjaw's realism.

It was half an hour after sun-up when Lance came back from the walk he had taken. He was carrying something under his coat and later was seen to transfer it to his saddle bags. He looked somehow more cheerful.

Doc Grimson eyed him shrewdly. "You've got some idea for trying to keep Lon from bein' killed," he charged.

Lance nodded. "Kind of," he acknowledged, but declined to say anything further. His idea didn't altogether suit his sense of fair play, so he preferred not to have the others know about it. That way, they wouldn't be responsible. Still, maybe it was more fair play than Canuck Bull deserved.... Anyway, it was the only thing Lance could think of which might save Lon Carmody's life.

They held their horses in readiness behind the hill where they could get to them without being seen when Slag McLeod appeared. That way they could take a slightly roundabout trail back to Jugtown.

"What if he doesn't come?" Lockjaw asked. "He'll maybe think we're lyin'."

"He'll come," Lance said. And Doc nodded agreement. Slag McLeod knew well enough that they were not liars.

It was mid-morning, however, before they saw the slender cloud of dust which marked a single rider. They waited until they could plainly make out the marshal's form, then, with a final glance to see that the guards were securely tied and the Chinamen safely locked up in their shack, they slipped out the back way to the horses. It would take brisk riding to get them to Jugtown by noon.

CHAPTER 14
HERO'S DRAW

JUGTOWN BUZZED with excitement. As the sun neared the zenith the main street looked as though there was a circus in town. Gun-fights were not new to Jugtown. There was usually one or two every Saturday night. It was a tough town. But this fight—if it came off—would be worth seeing!

All of the older residents knew the story of the licking that Lon Carmody had gotten and what it had done to his nerve. Seeing him go up against Canuck again was something that mustn't be missed.

Comment was about equally divided between skepticism

and amusement. Most people declared their belief that there was nothing in it. It was all a kind of joke. Others, who knew that Canuck had received a note in Lon's hand-writing, were inclined to believe that the bank teller had perhaps gone crazy enough to get himself killed. There wasn't much chance that he would really be able to down a man like Bull. Still, the mere fact that he was willing to try was enough to bring everybody out.

Jane Venner passed the morning in a state of almost intolerable nervousness. In her secret heart she had hoped for something like this, for Lon's sake. She knew that his life since Canuck had broken his nerve had not been worth living. But now that it was here, she would have given anything to be able to stop it. If Lon were killed…. Her heart grew cold and small within her at that thought.

Canuck Bull, curiously, was in his way almost as upset as Jane. The thing which was about to happen was inexplicable to him and so it got on his nerves. The note he had received had had a cold, threatening sureness about it which was hard to laugh off. And the mere fact that it had been written by anyone as harmless and craven as Carmody gave it a disturbing quality of unnaturalness. It was almost as though a kitten had suddenly begun to bellow like a bull.

Then, too, there was the possibility that the whole thing was a trick—a trick which might have something to do with the Five Mavericks. Bull and his men had acquired a healthy respect for those gentlemen during the past few days. And, apparently, the Mavericks had acquired some sort of animosity against

Bull and his army. Not content with shooting them up, they had come in and robbed the Palace of a large sum, and Canuck was not so stupid as not to see in that a special gesture directed at him. He had an idea that he hadn't seen the last of them, and the idea wasn't pleasant. No one before had ever gotten the better of him with such ease and consistency.

No, Canuck's nerve that morning, despite his bluster, had not been particularly good.

For all that, he was no coward and the idea that he might avoid being in front of the Palace at noon never occurred to him.

He was there, in fact, several minutes before the time, leaning with his back against the front of the building, surrounded by half a dozen of his hired gunmen and as many more of the tough characters of Jugtown who approved of his methods and profited by them.

Canuck laughed and joked with them in his customary hard, lusty way, but all the while his small black eyes, increasingly nervous, searched the street for the first sign of Lon Carmody. Suddenly he cursed and straightened. Five men had appeared across the street—five men whom he knew only too well. They had appeared, apparently, from nowhere and were leaning casually against the hitching rack in front of the general store. Evidently, they had seen him straighten and look at them, for they grinned at him mockingly, except for Lockjaw Johnson, who scowled belligerently. The big-shouldered young man who had knocked Canuck down—that was Clayton—looked at one of his companions and laughed, as though at some joke they shared between them.

Canuck hesitated. These were the men he had warned to leave town—the men who had responded by robbing his saloon. Their presence was open defiance and called for action. But the very openness of their presence and the casual confidence in their manner bluffed the boss of Jugtown for the moment. He suspected a trap. While he hesitated, the crowd down the street gave way hastily and Lon Carmody appeared, walking without haste and steadily in his direction.

Canuck pulled himself together and stepped out from his group, his eyes narrowing, head down a little, like a bull about to charge.

LANCE CLAYTON'S voice cut across the sudden silence that fell over the street. "We're seein' fair play here," Lance said. "This fight is between Lon Carmody and Canuck Bull. Anybody that tries to pull anything funny will have us to deal with."

Canuck growled, not taking his eyes from Carmody, "When this is over, we're gettin' you—and don't you forget it."

Lance Clayton laughed. "If you want your gang of scorpions to get us, Canuck, you better leave it in your will," he said mockingly. "When this is over, you'll be buzzard meat."

Lon Carmody came on steadily, until he was within ten paces of Canuck Bull. His face was pale, though two small spots of color glowed in his cheeks, and his eyes were glassy—expressionless.

Lance Clayton held his breath. He knew what an ordeal those hours of waiting must have been to Carmody. He had been afraid that the teller wouldn't show up at all. But he had thought that at the first sight of the other, he would be able to tell what Carmody was going to be able to do, whether he would lose his nerve and his head at the sight of Canuck or whether he would be able to make some sort of passable showing. Now, however, he found that he could read nothing in Carmody's face. He might be comparatively calm and determined or, he might be nearly paralyzed with fear. And in those seconds, Lance's pulses were jumping and racing as they never would have done if his own life had been at stake. Nervously, he felt under his coat for the thing he held there, feeling, as he did so, that so crazy an idea had no chance of working.

For what seemed a long time, Lon Carmody stood and stared at his enemy, and Bull, through narrowed eyes, stared at him. The crowd had given away, leaving a clear lane between the two men and the silence was absolute.

Then Canuck Bull spoke. His voice was a scornful bellow, but his eyes, Lance saw, were nervous: "Well, are you deaf and dumb, you dang yeller pup, or just skeered to death?"

Lon Carmody opened his mouth then. His voice came out of it, dead, expressionless: "You don't scare anybody, you bellowing bluff. I've waited three years to kill you an' now I'm goin' to do it. Fill your hand!"

As Carmody snapped out the last words, a squat, ugly-looking lizard—a good eighteen-inch specimen of chuckwalla—dashed out from somewhere and raced straight for Canuck Bull's legs. No one had noticed that Lance Clayton had stooped, just before the beginning of Carmody's speech, or that he had taken a fat chuckwalla from beneath his coat and, heading it in the direction of the boss of Jugtown, had struck a match on his finger-nail. Everyone had been too absorbed in watching the two men who confronted one another.

Canuck Bull had started his draw, his hand flashing toward the butt of his gun, when he saw the chuckwalla. He hesitated, then forgot everything for one fatal instant, as he stepped hastily out of the path of the lizard. It was not a long mistake, but it was a bad one. The big man caught himself together, white-faced, knocked off his base, first by the sight of the lizard and second by the realization that Carmody's gun was already leveled at him.

Too late, he drove again for his own gun. Knowing that unless Carmody missed, he was a dead man.

But Carmody did not fire! Instead, his voice whipped out: "Hold it! Hold your draw."

Dazed, Canuck Bull did so, just as his guns were clearing leather.

Lance Clayton groaned under his breath. The fool! The dam' honorable young fool!

He had lost his chance. Bull would kill him now, for sure.

"Leather your gun again," Lon Carmody snapped. "I'm killin' you, but I'm not killin' you that way." He holstered his own gun. "Now! Fill your hand!"

Together the two hands drove for gun-butts, but this time it was Canuck Bull's Colt which leveled first, thundered, spitting flame. But the shock to his nerves, already over-taut from suspense and worry, had told. He was pressing—trying to draw and shoot too fast. The slug snapped by Lon Carmody's leg. Then Carmody's gun roared, once—and again. Canuck Bull swayed backward and forward. Desperately he tried to raise his Colt to fire again, but could not. He sank to his knees, then toppled forward on his face.

Lon Carmody stood white-faced now—an expression of wonder, of unbelief, on his features. Stood until one of Canuck's henchmen made the mistake which started the holocaust—the mistake of diving for his guns.

Just what happened then the onlookers never knew. Two guns—those were Doc Grimson's—spoke from near the hitch-rack, and the henchman who had started his draw never finished it. Then the street was full of staccato thunder, of people racing for shelter against the blazing guns, of white smoke and the acrid stench of burnt powder.

WHEN THE smoke cleared, there were half a dozen bodies on the ground, but none of them were the bodies of the five men who had stood by the hitchrack. Those five men were still in much the same positions as before, holstering their smoking guns. In the middle of the street stood a blazing-eyed young man, powder-blackened, with blood on his cheek and blood staining his shoulder, and toward him ran Jane Venner, who had seen the whole affair from the window of the bank.

"Lon! Lon!" she cried, "you're hurt!" But Lon didn't look as though anything could ever hurt him. He gathered her into his arms, not even wincing at the pain in his shoulder.

Lance Clayton, watching, turned away. "So that job's done," he said matter-of-factly. "Let's go."

"Listen," Charlie Parr said grimly. "Now that this business is over, let's get going. This is the time to hit that bank."

Now that the shooting was over, the crowd had begun to gather again. One of the half a dozen figures on the ground stirred. It was Canuck Bull. He motioned to the Mavericks. Doc Grimson went to him, knelt at his side. The others followed.

"No," the big man gasped, "no use botherin'. I—I've got it—this time. I want to see Jane."

Lance went over and got Jane Venner and Lon Carmody.

Canuck Bull took the girl's hand. "Sorry—for everythin', Jane," he said. "Wanted to tell you—I'm leavin' everything—to you. Want you to—have the bank—everythin'." He turned his eyes feebly toward the crowd. "You hear—that, boys? That's my will—everythin' to Jane." He smiled a little at the girl "Some of it's not very—honest money—but you'll do good with it." He grinned. "I allus did want to do—somebody some good before I—died."

His head drooped suddenly and his eyes glazed. Canuck Bull had fought his last fight.

The Five Mavericks looked at one another in mute comprehension. Doc Grimson's eyes twinkled. "You heard him, Charlie." He nodded toward the grated windows of the building where Lon Carmody had once been teller and might now be president. "It belongs to her."

Charlie Parr threw up his hands, his face flushing with honest indignation. Then he turned and strode for his horse.

"Where you goin', Charlie," Lance asked, grinning.

Charlie glared at him. "I'm goin'," he exploded, "to find another bank, and stick it up!"

www.ingramcontent.com/pod-product-compliance
Lightning Source LLC
Chambersburg PA
CBHW071955170626
46813CB00005B/1895